Broken Petals

Inside the cracks of lust infused desires

Book Three in the Mated Fortune Series

J.P. Mooney

ISBN: 978-1-8380351-8-1

For more information:

www.jpmooneyliterature.co.uk

DEDICATION

To the broken lovers with hearts of steel.

CONTENTS

Chapter One

Isabella

It's you. It's always been you. The sun is shining in the bright blue sky, and the space between us has closed into unity. Even though we're far from innocent, the grass faintly smells like young love. Your smile is a flash of peace for me. A reserved balanced that I only dip into when necessary. Nonetheless, it's always a pleasure and a pain I'm willing to partake. So in this memory, I'll soak up the part of you that wanted to stay. The part of you that wanted me and the part of your heart that made me believe in love.

Every morning I wake up in a pool of sweat. My alarm nudged me into reality. My eyes struggled to open as tears crusted on my eyelashes. Even now, more so than ever, my need for solitude and freedom is intoxicating. My client list has remained exclusive, and I merely mingled with them as a means for escape. Frank is still my only trusted friend, and like myself, the torments of our past has catapulted us into indifference with the world. We accepted that we would never be normal and decided to throw our middle fingers up to life. While he amplified his dating contact list and pushed Mathew out of his memories, I boxed and worked out hard during the day and indulged in the ecstasy of aged bourbon at night. I chose to do anything and take everything that stopped my heart and mind from wondering at the stars looking for him. Ryan. I yearned for his warmth and his call. It's been eight months, and the ache is now a soft pull in my chest. It'll get better in time, but in the meantime, I'll self-nurse and medicate myself away from my reality. In my flat, I've found a deeper level of comfortability where I reside in a place of peace as my mind lingers in limbo between what has happened and what could be.

It's a cool Wednesday afternoon. I decided to have lunch with Frank since it was his day off. Since I only scheduled appointments with my clients only three times a week and the occasional weekend, I tried to stay active during the day to avoid falling deeper into depression.

"Your skin looks amazing, but your eyes are dull. I know you're broken right now, but you need to pull yourself together and move on." Frank said as he looked at the menu while I remained quiet and held on to my cup of coffee.

"Izzy, you're twenty-seven, and you're gorgeous. So what if he left? There are plenty of men out there for you. At the very least, find yourself someone hot to play with."

I respected Frank's honesty. But, it wasn't like me to let a man in and fall in love with him. And having a broken heart wasn't something I relished as part of my personality. So it was time for me to look forward to new opportunities and have some fun.

"You're right." I smiled as his eyes grew wide and quickly grabbed his hand before he could say anything else. "There's a new restaurant opening in Fitzrovia tonight. I received an invite from a client as a gesture of goodwill. We can go together and mingle, perhaps even look for some new clients, although I'm still debating this."

"Nice, I'll come to your flat after 5 p.m., and we can order the grandest taxi available. We both chuckled.

This was going to be a challenge as I hadn't ventured outside of my social circle in a while, but I was fabulous, and I knew I'd get used to being around new people soon enough. Lunch was at the local café, and it didn't take me long to walk home after Frank and I said our goodbyes. At home, I ran a rose bath and plunged my head in the water, letting my straight hair bounce back into its curls. Behind the blurriness of my wet eyelashes, memories of Ryan swished in my mind prompting my chest to collapse into an exhale. I was still so angry with him for leaving, but the truth is, my ego was hurt from his rejection. A man had never rejected me yet. He did. As I swirled the bathwater and lingered in my thoughts, I thought it would be good to research the restaurant opening and see who may be in attendance, but I decided against this as I thrilled off surprises. It was an odd day to have a restaurant opening, but I guessed that invitation was only given to a handful of people, my client George being one of them. He wasn't someone who loved to mingle and thought I would find the invitation more useful than himself.

At 5.30 p.m. I decided to wear a red pencil dress paired with nude pumps and a designer clutch Frank gifted me from one of his friend's boutiques in Chelsea. My hair was blow-dried into a sleek high ponytail, and my cheeks were contoured to the heavens. My signature scent for the night was a touch of Oudh musk strategically chosen to attract the highest quality attention. As I put the final touches of makeup and hairspray, Frank rang the doorbell.

"Let yourself in." We had matured to a place of trust, and we decided to cut each other a copy of our house keys to use in emergencies or with prior permission from one another. We had grown closer and had accepted each other as family, but that didn't mean that it was okay for either of us to take the piss and barge in unannounced. And I didn't worry about Frank going through my things because Nobody but myself had the combination for my safe that contained my work laptop, emergency cash and valuables.

"Wow, cheekbones night out." He teased. "You look amazing. I'm hoping we both get some tonight."

"Thank you, but tonight is about us having some fun. Let me know when you want to leave with or without me, and I'll be making my exit too. You look handsome too." I stood and looked at him for a moment. His muscles were still chiselled to perfection, visible and taut under his slim fit shirt and chinos. He grinned when he noticed my glare.

"This shirt is worth every penny I paid. Fancy a line before we leave?" I stood indecisive for a moment, trying to balance my desire to be carefree and my need for sensible sobriety. Most days, I had been indulging in joints and bourbon but compensated with cardio, kickboxing and staying hydrated, now it was time for us to socialise, and I was nervous.

"Fine, but only one to take the edge off." Thirty minutes later, we were grinning ear to ear as we climbed in and made our way to the restaurant.

"I hope the food is good. I'm starving." Frank whined.

"We can go somewhere else if it's not. Don't whine, you'll kill my buzz." I smirked. We arrived at the restaurant at 7 p.m. and headed to the chirpy receptionist.

"Good evening, welcome to GRACE, name please?"

"Isabella." She politely nodded and directed us to our table. The décor was not to my and Frank's taste, but it wasn't terrible. Pink velvet-lined furniture with silver trims fabric. The vibe was more suburban glitz than city chic. Nonetheless, we planned to stay for a few flutes of champagne and the food.

Most of the guests had already arrived, and the space was buzzing with light chatter and admiration. Some were genuinely curious and excited to be there, while others came to gloat in superiority and judgement. To our contentment, we were sat at a corner table that gave a view of the entire room. Ten minutes later, Frank and I were on our second flute of champagne, grazing on our hors d'oeuvre while the host and owner tapped his glass, summoning everyone to attention.

"Good evening, everyone. Welcome to Grace. My name is David. I am your host and partner. I hope you enjoy yourselves and are excited to sample the fabulous menu we have created. You will have an opportunity to speak with me throughout but in the meantime, please, relax while my team serves you." He gestured for the starters to be served, a mixture of fish, vegetarian, and meat tapas. Frank devoured them all while I stuck to the non-meat plates.

While Frank and the others focused on tasting the food and drinking, I focused on how handsome and young David looked; I guessed he was in his early 30s. And just as I was about to remark this to Frank, he appeared at our table with one of the most beautiful men I had ever seen. My eyes remained glued on both of them and the excitement I felt caught me off guard.
"Hello, I trust you are enjoying yourselves?" I remained stuck to my chair as Frank responded.

"Yes, everything is lovely. I'm Frank, and this is my friend Isabella." They exchanged handshakes while Frank discreetly nudged my side to bring back my attention.

"It's a pleasure to meet you." I gave them my best smile. "The food is great," I remarked awkwardly while David and the unknown beautiful man worked up their response.

"This is my business partner and younger brother, Nathan." I couldn't have guessed they were brothers since they looked nothing alike, although they were both handsome. Both David and Nathan continued to chat about the inspiration for the menu and the location. I tried to indulge in the conversation, but I must admit that I didn't care enough. The conversation eventually fizzled, and they moved on to the following table. Frank grinned like a Cheshire cat as he turned to analyse my frame.

"Seen someone you liked, did ya?" He kept his gaze on mine then broke into a laugh. "I don't blame you, Izzy. Nathan was hot. You should go and talk to him. I promise I won't leave without you unless you want me to." He raised his eyebrows in a conspiracy.

"He's hot, but no. We came here together to have a good time. I don't think talking to him will make the slightest difference to my life." He let the conversation slide, and we worked our way through the courses of our meal. By 9.30 p.m., the guests had diminished, and we decided it was our turn to leave. We said our thank you to David and the team, although Nathan was nowhere to be seen. Frank booked a taxi as we walked to the reception and saw Nathan chatting to the receptionist. His hair was short and curly, his shoulder broad and muscular under his slim fit shirt and his tanned skin glowed under the ambient light.

"Thank you for coming tonight; we hope to see you again." He grinned as we walked towards the door. The receptionist remained quiet while we bid our goodnights. The air between us felt awkward, and my instinct prompted my dislike for her. Frank flirtatiously spoke to Nathan, and I eventually had to pull him away.

"Well, he's very much into you Izzy, don't sleep on it." Frank said as we buckled our seatbelts and got comfortable. I smiled as the rate of my heartbeat picked up. I knew he was into me because I felt attracted to him too, but after protesting to frank earlier, there was no way I was going to admit it yet.

Since the night was still young, Frank and I decided to drink at our local bar. We ordered our usual bourbon to nurse the rest of the evening. However, as we sipped and chatted, I noticed the bar was busier than usual, with patrons celebrating a supposedly low key birthday dinner. As much as I wanted to stay and enjoy my drink, suddenly, I had an urge to go home.

"We just got here." Frank protested.

"And you can stay, I'm sorry, but I've reached my outdoor quota for today. I'll call you tomorrow." I kissed his cheek and placed some notes on the table to cover the drinks, and went home. My mind felt clearer as soon as I stepped on the pavement, and I took a slow deep breath savouring the crisp air before I set my stride home. As I approached my flat building, I ceased when I saw Nathan walking towards me. It was 10.30 p.m., his shirt was messy, and his eyes reflected exhaustion. Still, my stomach got nervous.

"Well, hello again. Where are you off to?" He said with a cunning smile that some men had used and gotten me into trouble before.

"Just going home." I smiled back.

"It seems that I'd be seeing you often. I also live nearby."

And before I knew it, I was in his living room with a glass of bourbon. Nathan's house was a few minutes' walk from my flat, and when he had suggested we have a drink together, I knew that I wanted to be outrageous yet again. So we talked and strolled to his townhouse, which was quite an odd choice in Shoreditch. I learned that both he and David were chefs; however, they decided it would be easier to stick to managing the restaurant and only help in the kitchen when necessary as they trusted their team.

He was thirty-one years old, and David, thirty-five. My cheeks heated when he looked at me as we both sipped our bourbons, but I managed to keep my cool.

"Have you lived here long?" I asked.

"No, just moved in a month ago. I lived with David before in Fitzrovia, but it was time to get some space. You?"

"I've been here just over a year now. The area has a nice vibe."

"So, what do you do for work?" The inevitable question. I was such a professional that it became second nature to navigate this question with finesse. From assessing his house and his business, I knew he was financially stable but definitely couldn't afford my services regularly unless he was secretly wealthy. Externally, he seemed to be doing well for himself at his age. Still, I usually provided my service to men who had done exceptionally well in business and were merely looking for some fun. I opted for the straightforward approach to give him the standard half-truth answer. I wanted to have some fun with him without complication and drama.

"I run a successful blog for interior design, connecting businesses and designers for collaborations." He looked curious yet, impressed. This was the usual reaction with regular men I've met. They usually felt at ease with a woman who was doing well in business yet, wasn't at their level. If I had said that I was wealthy and barely worked, they'd usually disengaged and became suspicious. This is one of the reasons why I rarely dated for relationships.

"I love creative people. There's no limit to the imagination."

He smirked as he slowly leaned forward to kiss me. It was nothing like how I imagined it to be. I thought that the butterflies in my stomach were from my attraction to him, and I thought it would be fiery, yet it wasn't. As our mouths enveloped each other's lips and our tongues entwined, my mind was racing with options. I could break the kiss and leave or stay and see how far I was willing to go. Nathan didn't repulse me, and there was nothing wrong with him. Although the chemistry was now lacklustre still, I chose to stay. Our kiss deepened as we raced to remove each other's clothes, and I immediately felt glad I stayed. His abs were chiselled to perfection, and the muscles on his arms were taut and smooth. Every inch of my body was awakened as his hands glided down my chest and roamed over my breasts. His lips were soft and warm on my neck. We explored each other's bodies for a while until he slid inside me and sunk his teeth into my neck. It was a welcomed pain, and I allowed myself to surrender to his pleasure. No words were muttered between us, just the sounds of our breathing and our touch. We fucked like teenage lovers reuniting for the first time like we knew the sky would open and the earth would finally fall into its demise. We succumbed to the ecstasy and eventually fell on our backs on the living room floor, hearts beating and sweat beads on our bodies. He leaned on his side and stroked my cheeks. I was awakened. The moment was short-lived when my phone buzzed a message from Frank.

I knocked for you, but you weren't there. Let me know if you're okay.

I'm fine. Speak tomorrow. X

Nathan had gone to the kitchen for some water, and I took the opportunity to get dressed quickly and gathered my bag. The moment we shared was nice. Still, it was a one-night stand, and I never did the walk of shame. It was best to make my exit gracefully.

"You're not staying the night?"
"No, I have to be up early tomorrow. I'll see you around." There was a beat of silence between us before he walked to the coffee table and grabbed a business card.

"I'd like to see you again. Here's my number." I hesitated to take the card for a moment, but the thought of seeing him again had crossed my mind. I shoved the card in my bag and swiftly made my exit leaving the trail of my fragrance behind. Thankfully the taxi I had booked while Nathan was in the kitchen was already parked outside. When I arrived home, I went straight for the shower and tossed my clothes in the laundry bin. I got into my nightdress and drank a bottle of water before climbing into bed.

Chapter Two

Isabella

My alarm pulled me out of sleep at 9 a.m. The sun flooded my bedroom through the curtain, and surprisingly, my cocooned emotions from the past few months had lifted. I felt lighter and energised as I rolled out of bed with the motivation to go for a long run. After I freshened up and changed into my workout kit, the memory of the night before tapered in my mind prompting a smirk. Then, I remembered that Nathan had given me his business card, although I hadn't decided if I wanted to see him again.

Going for a run, I'll come by at lunchtime.

Okay, let yourself in.

I knew that Frank would be excited to hear about my shenanigans but, I noted that I would bring him some lunch to make up for ditching him at the bar. I saw the same familiar faces going about their daily routines on my way to the park. The only face I didn't see since Ryan left was Juliana's. His perfect sweet friend who could do no wrong. I had paid one of Frank's guys to see if she was still residing in the area, and they reported that she had moved out a while ago. I chose not to intrude on her life, considering I spiked her drink to get her talking and thought it was best to let her be. She wasn't harmful to Frank and me, and frankly, I knew that we would have never been real friends. She was too sweet. I don't mean the type of edge that hid behind innocence. She was really innocent and sweet despite her courage to deal with Andrew, justified. I would've personally dealt with him less delicately, although I *really* did, eventually. I continued running until my heart raced and my lungs begged for oxygen. This was when I pushed myself even harder to get all toxicity out of my mind, body and spirit. I used to hate running until I noticed the subtle ways it helped my body release what I didn't need, and it kept my legs toned and lean. I eventually arrived home an hour later and jumped in the shower while I was still pumped with adrenaline. It was just after 1 p.m. when I arrived at Frank's apartment dressed in white trousers and a simple satin blouse. He emerged from his room with a vape.

"You said we were having lunch."

"Yes, but it's also my day off, and I need a little pick me up. So where would you like to eat?" He grinned as he walked to the kitchen and poured us both some juice.

"The patisserie around the corner will suffice. I need carbs and sugar. Speaking of sugar, last night was interesting." I giggled.

"Oh, dear, who was it?" Frank asked deadpanned as he inhaled his vape and took a sip of his juice. I couldn't keep a straight face for fear of telling him that he was right about Nathan, but the experience was too good not to tell him.

"Nathan." He gasped and exhaled a deep laugh. "I knew it! I fucking knew it. You were silently swooning when he came to our table, and I knew you made a lasting impression on him. How was he?" We both laughed while my cheeks burned.

"At first, it was pleasant. I almost changed my mind, but then it felt great. Obviously, it was just a one-night thing, but it was so needed." I chirped as we made our way out the door towards the patisserie. Frank listened intently as he floated in the ecstasy of his earlier vaping activities.

"Well, it's about time you let a man in down there. I assumed it was starting to get dusty." I smacked his shoulder as he laughed like a naughty teenager. We arrived at the patisserie and ordered a sandwich, each with a chocolate cake to share. It was a dry Thursday, and so far, I had nothing planned, so I thought it would be a good idea to spend the day with Frank. I suggested we go shopping and see where the day took us.

"Izzy, we both know that shopping is a bad idea when I'm high and you're not. You're going to control everything, and I'm going to sink in my careless mood." I frowned, unamused.

"We'll be fine. All you have to do is accompany me and sit on the nice velvet sofas until I'm done. Deal?"

"Fine. But I don't want any fuss." He smiled, knowing that he was never going to win. I decided to browse the boutiques on Shoreditch High Street, where I bought two cashmere jumpers and skinny jeans. Even though it was spring, I thought that I could never have enough jumpers since I was always cold once autumn fell. We walked down Brick Lane, and I bought Frank two minimalist ornaments for his apartment since he was exceptionally patient in the boutiques.

An hour later, we were browsing the work of a young artist in the local gallery. I wasn't keen on the pieces, but Frank was convinced that he saw the more profound meaning they were trying to convey. We walked around with our arms locked in each other's when I saw Nathan talking to the receptionist. She was pretty and petite, and he seemed very interested in what she had to say. I subtly nudged Frank's arm to a halt.

"That's your fling, isn't it." He whispered.

"Yes, shit. Quickly, let's leave."

"The only way out is past them, don't be immature. Just carry on minding our business." He pulled my arm, and we walked towards the last painting. "Excuse me, I would love to know more about this piece. Do you mind?" Frank announced the receptionist prompting both her and Nathan in our direction. I was annoyed, but I carried on as if I hadn't seen them first.

The receptionist walked over and spoke to Frank for a few minutes while Nathan gave me a small wave. I didn't want to see him again this soon, let alone in a gallery, but I had no choice but to be courteous and say hello. I looked over at Frank, who was busy chatting away giggling and knew that we wouldn't be leaving for at least another ten minutes.

"Hi, fancy seeing you here. We seem to like a lot of the same places." His grin was warm and friendly. It's crazy to think that we were enveloped in each other's arms a few hours ago, and now we were standing there talking like strangers.

"Hi, I'm here with a friend. How are you?" It dawned on me that I shouldn't have mentioned that Frank was a friend. I should've made him wonder if he would be competition. And knowing Frank, Nathan wouldn't stand a chance. I grinned at myself with the thought. Perhaps I could find someone else to make him jealous if whatever we had between us went further.

"I'm fine. How about I take you on a date." He paused and grabbed my eyes with his. "Not at my restaurant. Somewhere we've both never tried." We lingered for a moment, and I had to hide my smile behind my game face. "Tomorrow night then?"

"Okay. I'll text you my number."

"You can do it now. That way, I know you're serious." He smirked.

I punched his number on my phone as he recited the digits since I hadn't brought his business card with me. Just as we finished, Frank walked overlooking cheery with his new art. Both men acknowledged each other with a hello, but I nudged Frank to leave Nathan behind with the gallery receptionist for our swift exit.

"Be careful with this one Izzy, judging by how the receptionist swooned over him, women must fall at his feet." Frank laughed. Behind that laugh, though, I knew what he meant. My need to control the situation may get out of hand, and Frank knew it too.

It was nearly dinner time when we arrived at Frank's apartment, so we ordered Japanese food for dinner. Frank's high had subsided, and I was rather proud of myself to be sober, not that there was any reward to cope with life sober. After dinner, we were in our usual ritual laying next to each other in bed, discussing our plans for the upcoming months. We played with the idea of taking a trip to Norfolk, an attempt to disconnect from the chaotic jungle of city life. The thought soothed and calmed me until I closed my eyes and saw him. Ryan.

Chapter Three

Isabella

Friday evening had arrived, and I was getting ready for my date with Nathan. He decided to take me to Boukan, a newly opened restaurant near London Bridge. I checked the menu online, and it consisted of various world dishes. I thought it was a safe move for him since he didn't yet know what I liked. The bar looked good, although I didn't plan to get tipsy. I opted for a pair of nude pointed heeled pumps and a slim fit dress. Simple yet elegant enough to make a lasting impression. The taxi arrived at 7 p.m. as I noticed my stomach began to knot. Unusual since I didn't think I liked him much. The night we spent together was fun; however, I certainly wasn't looking for a relationship.

I walked up the stairs and entered Boukan, which was a lot nicer than its pictures. The receptionist guided me to our table. Nathan looked a lot sharper than our previous reunions. His shirt was crisp, hair smoothed, exhibiting his piercing brown eyes. His cologne seduced my nose. I wanted to pull him closer to me for a deeper sniff, but that would've been weird. I realised the beat between us had lingered a little longer than it should have, so I said hello and took my seat. If Nathan was nervous, he didn't let it show, and I was determined to keep myself together.

"Wine?" He smiled as though he heard my thoughts.

"I would love to try the Grenache." I smiled as sweetly as I could. I felt like we were playing a game that I didn't know the rules of, but it could've been his upfront exterior. Regardless, I wasn't letting my guard down.

Dinner was quiet. We managed a few cheeky jokes, and he was undoubtedly a handsome man, while he lacked the edge I was usually drawn to.

"Not how you expected I would be?" His words pulled me out of my thoughts.

I hesitated. "It's okay if I'm not your type. I'm happy you gave me a chance, though." He looked at the waitress and requested another whiskey.

"I'm complicated." I blurted. The truth was, I almost wished he was my type. Sweet and simple.

"We all have some complications. I mean, I'm not perfect despite my charming exterior." If only he knew how heartless I was. Now more than ever. "Why do you think you're so undeserving of having this?"

He held my hand and my eyes in his.

I hesitated and looked at the beautiful view on the horizon. He placed his hand on my cheek and traced his finger down to tip my chin up to him.

"Try me." For a split second, I thought about telling him everything. I wanted to rip my chest open, take my heart and hand it to him to fix it. I was so broken that I didn't even know if it could be whole again. "I'm not going to hurt you." His words snapped me out of his trance. As much as I wanted to believe him, I knew that I didn't and couldn't because that would mean putting my guard down for a complete stranger.

"I'm going to order another drink. Then we're going back to your place. If you want to." He sat back and bit his lip. His eyes danced with a dare to keep pushing, but I knew how to push back, and he would lose. He smiled and signalled the waitress for another drink.

One hour later, we stumbled through his front door with our lips locked onto one another. His hands roamed my body, exploring every curve while his tongue tasted the perfume on my neck. As the familiar sensation crept up and down my spine, I let my mind wander to the memory of the familiar touch of my love.

"Who broke you?" Nathan breathed in between the kisses that threatened to intoxicate me. Our mating dance led us to his bedroom, where I took a seat on the edge of his bed. We stared at each other for a moment. His gaze dared me to try and scare him with my scars. I refused.

"You have to let this go. Let's have fun and enjoy each other's company, nothing more." He smiled and stroked my cheek. "I hate it when you do that."

"This must be our first-ever fight." He broke into laughter. "Who fights in the middle of being seduced anyway?" He laughed again.

Then it hit me that Nathan wanted more than I was willing to give. "There is no we." I stood up to leave, but he gently touched my arm and asked me to stay. His eyes were dark and exciting. I leaned in and kissed him deeply until we both sunk into his bed. The first time, we fucked like horny teenagers, but this time it meant more than just a moment of satisfaction. Something ticked inside me, and he opened a wormhole of possibilities, unlocking a thirst for his body that I didn't know I had. We made love in another dimension, exploring every single inch of our bodies synchronised together in one beat. It felt incredible and too comforting.

Two hours later, we were resting side by side with our eyes still locked onto each other. "See, you say there's no we, but we're so drawn to each other."

"What is your game?" I snapped back and was met with a confused face. "I told you where we stood. There is no we. If you can't handle that, then this is the last time you'll see me."

"There is no game. I just like you. Is that a crime?"

I pulled myself out of bed and got dressed. It was time for me to get out of there before it got too complicated.

"Look, I'm sorry if I scared you by coming on too strong. I'm just upfront, and I don't like to play games." He followed me towards the front door.

"Nothing scares me, Nathan." I left his house before he had a chance to respond. It was a shitty move on my part, and he hadn't done anything wrong, but his questioning was getting me close to my rage. I hated it when men felt like they could push my boundaries. No meant no.

I arrived home at 10.30 p.m., relieved to find some leftover pasta in the fridge as I was starving. My adrenaline had reduced, but I was still annoyed at the situation. Since it was still early, I made my way to Frank's apartment. I needed the sanity and reasoning of my best friend.

"What did he do?" Frank said as he enveloped me in his arms.

"We look ridiculous like this. You're so big, and I'm tiny next to you" I managed a soft laugh. I told him everything, and he listened intently. Frank didn't judge.

I woke up on Frank's empty bed to find a note next to my pillow.

Gone to work. Stay for the day if you want, we'll hang out later.

I didn't mean to stay the night, but we carried conversation until I crashed and knowing Frank, he would have vaped himself to sleep in front of the TV. I rolled out of bed and headed into the bathroom. Frank was immaculately clean for a man, especially now that he was single. I jumped in the shower to wash the funk from the night before. Nathan's behaviour still grated my skin, and even though he was a good fuck, I knew that things had to stay exactly how they were. How needy did one need to be? He barely knew me, and I'm sure he would run a mile if he got to. It was time for me to avoid him at all costs now before things got sticky as they usually did. I towelled dry, moisturised and wore the spare clothes I kept at Frank's for emergency sleepovers. One thing I never did was the walk of shame. I pulled my hair in a high bun, made Frank's bed and headed home.

Didn't mean to intrude and crash last night but thanks for not kicking me out :)

I messaged Frank

Don't be ridiculous. Dinner and drinks tonight. I'm tired already.

Okay xx

I would choose a night out with Frank over a date any day, except if the date was paying a load of cash. I bought some pastries from the local bakery and checked my phone as my bites matched my steps on the way home.

Voicemail: *Hi Isabella…I hope you got home okay. I'm sorry for how the night ended.*

Voicemail: *Look, at least message me to let me know you got home okay.*

My heart sunk for a bit. He seemed genuinely worried, but he didn't have to be. I knew how to look after myself. Like he asked, I dropped him a text to let him know I was okay. He didn't respond. Fine. It was 8 a.m. when I arrived at my apartment. My favourite place in the world. I had the day to myself, and I was out of my routine. It made me anxious, especially since I didn't have any clients booked in until the following week. I rummaged through my safe, counted the cash, gold bars, and checked my go bag and documents to ensure everything was still in place. Everything I needed to start a new life was in that safe. I had made arrangements for Frank too, just in case he needed it but should the unfortunate happen, I promised that I wouldn't force him to come with me unless he wanted to.

By 10 a.m., restlessness had settled in, so I got in my workout kit and went for a run. Despite the light drizzles of rain, I did my usual route that threatened my curls to frizz. I pushed myself even further into my stride until I collapsed on my living room floor, drenched in sweat. After my second shower of the day, I was famished. I ordered sushi for lunch and indulged in my meal on the balcony. The spring breeze breathed life into the city, and I was grateful to still be alive. The memory of my past had never left me, but I was determined to have a good life and live it my way.

"Well you've been productive, I see. You're glowing," Frank remarked from the doorway. "Good run?"

"Indeed. Your portion is in the fridge." I gestured mid-chew of my tuna roll. He displayed a grateful nod, grabbed his food and joined me.

"Has he called you yet?"

"Left two voicemails last night asking to let him know I got home okay. So I messaged him this morning."

"Urgh, so needy." Frank laughed. "He obviously likes you, Izzy. Maybe you need to open up to him a bit. Sure, he seems sickly sweet from what you've told me but do you blame him?" We both giggled.

"I know, I'm a dish, but I'm not ready for anything serious. I just want to have fun."

"Okay. So, we're going to Chelsea tonight for some fun. Work's been so boring. Lately, I need to let loose and have a good fuck." I looked at him with embarrassment at the sound of those words. Yes, we were very close and lived life on the edge, but I certainly didn't need to hear him say he needed a good fuck. He started laughing out loud as though he had read my mind.

"Oh, calm down, Izzy, you've done worse." I giggled out loud because it was indeed true. Frank never failed to make me laugh, and I was eternally grateful that he had been my rock throughout the past few months.

We sat on the balcony for a while and watched the world go by as we chatted about life. Then we progressed to getting ready and agreed to meet at his apartment at 7 p.m. I decided to go all out in a bodycon dress and barely-there heels with my hair straightened down my back. Frank wore his usual black fitted shirt, trousers and shoes. Simple yet sexy as always. We had a glass of wine in his kitchen and shared a joint before we headed for a restaurant called *Click*.

"Really?" I turned to Frank, who appeared on cloud nine with pupils as big as a goldfish.
'Yeah, apparently, this is where people come to click with each other." He laughed really loud that people turned to look.

We were sat at a corner table on the terrace that overlooked the city lights. Faint daylight beamed on the horizon, but my skin prickled with the chilly air. Frank had brought his jacket draped over my shoulders as we sipped our red wine.

"I am well buzzed and optimistic right now."

"I can see that." I unintentionally snorted in my glass. My high had crept up so suddenly that I barely held an appetite, although I was accustomed to how quickly our nights out unravelled. I forced myself to have a few slices of pizza. Frank was in a world of his own, and I had to admit that this was the kind of night I had been craving. Although I had enjoyed my responsible routine, the monstrous side of me was daring to come out and play. I took another sip of my wine, and Frank topped it up with a smirk. We ate, sipped and talked for a while until the familiar face that walked through the terrace door broke my high.

"Shit, it's Nathan." Frank turned around and gave a noticeable look. "Fuck. He's with someone. Let's leave."

"What's the problem? You said you didn't want him like that." The sound of his words didn't match the movement of his mouth. I didn't care that Nathan was there with another woman. I just didn't want to have a conversation with him while inebriated.

"No, but I'm so faded." I exaggerated a whisper. Frank agreed to pay the bill as soon as we finished our pizza and drinks. His smile was now a frown as we headed for the exit.

"We didn't even get to have dessert." He pouted. "I've been tanking my workouts this week, and I really wanted dessert." I tried to hold in my laugh.

"I'm sorry, boo. I'll make it up to you." We walked swiftly by Nathan's table and made our way to the foyer before he noticed where I agreed to wait while Frank used the bathroom. Ten seconds later, Nathan approached the foyer.

"I thought that was you." Fuck.

"Hi, just leaving. Enjoy your evening." That was mean, but I really couldn't have a friendly conversation with him when my devilish side was creeping near the surface. He politely agreed and walked back to his date. Who leaves their date to chase a woman in a restaurant anyway? I continued to look over at them, all smiles and dimples. I bet she was a solicitor or something dull. Regardless, I just wanted to have fun tonight. He leaned in and whispered in the solicitor's ear the way he did to me the night before. My stomach dropped. Jealousy spiked through me like a stake in a vampire's heart.

"Oh, don't you flip out on me right now." Frank wrapped his arm around my shoulders in preparation for my upcoming rage. But, instead, I stormed out of the restaurant and opened my nostrils to the fresh air as we stepped on the pavement.
"This is fucking hilarious. You don't want him, but you don't want anyone else to have him." Frank chuckled. It was contagious, and my rage subsided. Fuck it, I was ready to have fun. We hid under a smoking shelter by the side of the restaurant and shared another joint. The flame

burnt my lungs as the smoke clouded my mind into euphoria.

"Let's go!"

Chapter Four

Frank

Izzy grabbed my hand and led me down the street to a club. Seeing her get jealous overseeing Nathan with another woman was funny. I didn't really trust Nathan, but I knew Izzy could look after herself. She hated when I got overprotective and was better off learning from her mistakes in her own time. It was just after 10.15 p.m., but the queue wasn't too bad. We eventually managed to grab a table close to the bar and ordered two bourbons. I lived for nights out with Izzy. No pressure, no judgements and no emotions. Just fun and games. We drank and danced until I spotted my liaison for the night.

"I'm Hugh. How's it going?" He was handsome and forthcoming.

"Frank." He ordered me and Izzy a round of drinks while making himself and his friend comfortable around our table. Hugh's wingman chatted to Izzy as we flirted with each other. "Do you live nearby?" I asked teasingly.

We looked over at Izzy, swaying to the music and laughing with Hugh's friend. "Go, I'll message you when I get home." She mouthed with a wink.

Hugh's flat was dimly lit and tidy. He poured us some whiskey that further fuelled my need for a release. I gulped the golden elixir in one go before my lips leeched onto his mouth and made their way around his neck. He reciprocated the action but took my hand and led me to his bedroom. In that moment, each piece of our clothing dropped to the floor until we both stood in our naked perfection. Hands roaming and exploring as our mouths breathed lustful breaths.

We fucked like it was the first and last time we saw each other because it was just that. Hugh was a beautiful man, but my deepest scar felt exposed even here, at my highest. Things didn't just change for Izzy in the past months. I needed her just as much as she needed me. The debacle with Mathew broke me. He was my first real love and possibly my last. To top it all, I couldn't walk through life pretending that I didn't kill a man. It was an accident; nonetheless, we covered it up like a crime. No conversation or query around Darrian's disappearance had surfaced, and I followed up with the guys to ensure not a single trace of him was left behind. I trusted that I was safe, but the memories and guilt swelled behind the darkness of my eyelids. So I savoured the moments of lustful pleasures to numb my pain.

I left Hugh's flat at 3 a.m. and headed to Izzy's apartment. My high had subsided by the time I reached her building, where I unsurprisingly saw Hugh's friend making his way towards the train station. I waited until he was out of sight before walking inside the building.

"Well, I'm glad we both had some fun." I said as I walked down the corridor towards her living room, where she reclined in her fancy kimono.

"Looks that way." She giggled.

Our nights out together would sometimes end with us relaxing on the bed or sofa, but this was the first time we both ended up with someone, and I made my way back to her. She was a comfort blanket, the sister and mother I never really had. She put out a fresh towel and some fresh loungewear I occasionally left there.

"Have a shower, drink some water, and we'll talk in the morning. I'm tired."

So I did.

My eyes tore open as the memory of the night before descended into a smile. I turned on my side to check on Izzy, but she was absent. I figured she was probably preparing breakfast. I rolled out of bed, staggered to the bathroom for a shower, and brushed my teeth. It had just gone 10 a.m. by the time I emerged in the living room that presented an empty coldness. Confused, I looked for Izzy in each room and the balcony, but she was definitely not in the apartment.

Where are you??

"You're finally up!" She announced as she walked through the front door with her phone in hand. "I got us some breakfast and fancy coffees." She smiled and walked to the kitchen.

"You could've nudged me awake. I was mildly worried." I chuckled.

We carried our chatter as we ate our breakfast and laughed about the previous night's shenanigans.

"I think you should give Nathan another chance." I blurted in between sipping my coffee. She gave me a fiery stare that prompted me t tread the subject carefully. "I mean, I know our lives are fucked, and we're pretty fucked up people, but that doesn't mean that you shouldn't be happy. You've been glowing the past few days."

"How can I bring myself to trust someone after Ryan? The way he left me despite my pleading." Her eyes threatened to tear up, and my instinct was to neutralise it with a hug. I had never seen my best friend break like this. She was a force to be reckoned with, and she deserved to be happy regardless of circumstances. Hell, if I was into women, I would've married her by now. I smiled into her neck at the thought.

"I'm not saying you elope and marry the guy right now. Just give him a chance and have some fun. You're practically free to do whatever the hell you want now. Stay focused on making money but have some fun. Besides, I always have your back if things get rough. Just have some fun, Izzy." I held her gaze for a moment.

"People always die when I have fun." She sighed. Her attempt at making a joke signalled my success in convincing her. We both laughed and continued to talk until lunchtime, when I decided to go home. She invited me to stay for Sunday lunch, but I was still satisfied with breakfast and needed a long workout with an even longer nap. Nevertheless, I left her apartment with a deep feeling of belonging and was very grateful for our friendship.

After the gym, I headed back upstairs to my apartment and immersed my body under the jets of the shower. As I lathered, I thought about my own relationships. I had cut ties with everyone, especially Mathew. After the Darrian debacle and moving apartments, I needed a fresh start. At this stage in my life, I needed to evaluate my desires. Being in a relationship wasn't for me until I met Mathew, but his betrayal taught me a valuable lesson. To always keep my freedom and not lose myself. Life had been quite simple and somewhat boring over the past few months. Izzy and I have been cautious and reserved. Last night had reignited my thirst for being out and about until I slept with Hugh. It seemed like a good idea at the time, but now that the weed and alcohol had dissipated from my system, it felt dirty and cheap. I had an itch that needed to be scratched as usual, and this time around, I was still unsatisfied. After my shower, I lounged in bed and felt safe enough to bring out an old phone from the safe. I turned it on and listened to the voice messages I had always dreaded to hear.

In Devon. Is she okay?
> *It's been three weeks, and I haven't heard from you. Just let me know Isabella's okay.*

Before Ryan left, he gave me a phone to keep in contact so that he could occasionally check on Izzy. I felt guilty keeping this from her, but it was a necessary evil to help her move on. He didn't want to leave her but felt that it was the right thing to do. They needed space from each other, and his life was even more fucked up than ours. I made him a promise to let him know that she was okay. After that, our communication was no more than a call, message or voicemail here and there.

Yes, she's moving on slowly but surely.

I typed with a heavy heart.

Good.

I turned the phone off and placed it back in the safe. I rolled on my side and slept for the rest of the afternoon.

The sound of my ringing phone pulled me out of deep sleep. My open curtains let the darkness and glare from the streetlight trickle through the windows. The phone vibrated on my bedside table as I struggled to adjust my vision.

"Frank!" I widened my eyes as I heard Izzy's voice. She was frantic and screechy before the line went dead. I called her back, but there was no answer. *What was that?* I climbed out of bed and got dressed. I tried calling her back, but the phone went straight to voicemail. Without hesitation, I headed straight for the door towards her apartment. By the time I reached her building, I had halted with caution in case there were unwanted visitors, but I quickly decided to double my pace towards her door with the key dangling in my hand. I let myself in with caution, to *unsurprisingly* see traces of blood smeared across her floor. *Don't let this be what I hope it's not.* I mentally plead to the universe. I walked into the living room with purpose to find Isabella sitting on the sofa holding a glass of bourbon while covered in blood. She had purple bruises on her neck and scratches on her cheek. My heart raced, and my mind clouded with questions, but I was relieved that she was alive. Her eyes were dark and thirsty for revenge and violence. I knew that look. I knew that this was unprovoked, and her monster had been awakened once more.

I sat next to her and took a sip from her glass, eager to take the edge off while my eyes traced the blood from the hallway, which eventually led to behind the sofa. Then, astounded, I saw the familiar body and face from the night before. Hugh's friend. I turned my body to face Izzy, who was now strangely calm.

"He came back here and tried it with me. I told him to leave, but he forced his way in to attack me hence the marks." She gestured to her face and neck. "I was really trying to not do this again, Frank. He was going to assault me." My anger rose with the pace of my breath. If she hadn't killed him, I definitely would have. "I shouldn't have brought him back here. I broke my own rule."

"No! Don't you dare say that. And don't you dare think for a second that this was your fault. We went out and had fun like anyone else. He brought this on himself. We sat in silence for a moment, contemplating our next steps, but I already knew what I needed to do. There was no question about it. Izzy was my best friend, and we protected each other. I made a call to the guys while she emerged from her bedroom with a handful of cash. I doubted we were the most handful out of the guys' customers, but we were indeed the most expensive, although we always paid our debt.

Thirty minutes later, the body was removed, and the blood had been professionally cleaned with special chemicals to leave the apartment traceless. I didn't even bother to know his name, but Izzy did and wanted the memory to evaporate. We lay in her bed with a glass of wine, each sharing a joint like it was a cheesy gangster movie. Although our lives weren't cheesy, and we were far from gangsters. We were criminals. That was the truth. We spent the rest of the evening in a wine haze as the high from the smoke subsided, leaving our insides sizzling with acute calmness. I nursed Isabella's face with antiseptic and tiny plasters that managed to cover the scratches and cuts. The bruise on her neck had grown darker, and I knew that it would only look worse before it got better. She had since showered and wrapped her long hair in a bun that exposed her high cheekbones. Her eyes, tired and jaded, threatened unpredictability every time they met mine. She had opened herself up to opportunities and shone her light; however, I, of all people, should've known that her light was too bright. She attracted the best and the worst of men. They got addicted and crazy after being with her. I wrapped my arms around her shoulders and held her tight. Her body remained stiff and her aura cold.

"I'm sorry I wasn't here, Izzy." I kissed the top of her head.

"It could've happened at any time. I'm glad you're here now." She released herself from my hold and walked straight to bed, where I followed behind. She lifted the covers and climbed underneath as I grabbed a blanket from the cupboard and headed towards the sofa. I wanted to be her comfort, but I also knew that she needed her space. I was not her romantic partner, and I had to uphold and respect her boundaries. "See you in the morning." She said as though reading my thoughts.

"Call me if you need anything."

I retired to the comfort of the sofa, but my mind and heart were nowhere from feeling comforted. I thought about all the eventualities that could've occurred, and I grew agitated. Then I thought about Hugh. Perhaps he would've wondered where his friend went. The guys had taken care of our mess before without leaving any connections to us, but this was different. Hugh was a stranger, and so was his friend. There's no way we could completely cover our tracks. People saw us together at the club, and eventually, someone would talk when his family reported him missing. Shit. My mind spun in questions for hours until I eventually fell asleep. By morning, I turned abruptly on the sofa to see Isabella standing at the kitchen island peeling and preparing fruits for the juicer. She quickly noticed my gaze and smiled. "Green or berry?" She offered. "Green, always. Thank you." I walked into the kitchen to her. She stayed calm even though I could sense her anxiety matched mine. We drank our juice in silence and went about the rest of our day encased in unspoken questions. By the time Monday morning arrived, I had made myself a small cocoon on Izzy's sofa. I didn't want to leave her alone and thought that if anyone came looking for trouble, it would've been best for everyone if I was to avoid another unnecessary murder. The tension in my shoulders alerted my awareness to what a shitty start to the workweek it would be, and I was sure Izzy had felt the same.

"I was up all night thinking about it." She walked in with her mouth moving quickly to push out the words. "It's not the fact that I killed him. I mean, yes, I was trying to be good, but I've gotten used to killing." I looked up at her dilated pupils, astounded. What the fuck did she take?

"Okay." I cleared my throat as I rolled myself up from the sofa.

"It's the fact that I wasn't in control. He almost had me, Frank!" I continued to stare at her without blinking. It was 6 a.m., and I was never ready for this type of morning chatter. "It's like he made me kill him, and there was no thrill. Just pure survival mode, and I hate that. There was no money at stake, just possibly my life, and I hated that the feeling reminded me of how mortal I am. Yuck.' She sat in the fancy velvet armchair, and we both stared at each other. Her, waiting for me to respond, and I, well, I was confused as fuck. I cleared my throat again as I tried to manifest my response.

My mouth opened to form the shape of words, but nothing came out. I tried again. "Erm, are you on some uppers?" Of all the questions, I chose this to possibly piss her off. "I mean, it's okay if you are, but I just need to make sure that you're okay and took it for the right reason." My mouth curved into a semi worried smile.

"Well, yeah, and I had a can of energy drink to keep me up because I didn't sleep properly. Way too many questions swirling up there." She gestured her finger in a circular motion at her head. Her come down would hit her like a ton of bricks. I guess it was a great day to call in sick from work as I couldn't leave her like this.

Izzy's fidgety mood had left me mildly annoyed yet amused all morning. She asked a few questions to mostly answer it herself while I nursed myself with pastries, water and coffee to keep me focused. By 9 a.m. I decided to shower and change into fresh clothes while trying to curve my appetite for the gym. I made a mental note to go after Izzy had fallen asleep. For now, I just had to make sure she survived the rest of the day. A loud thud at the door jerked me out of my thoughts. I rushed to the kitchen to check on her, but Izzy was just as surprised as I was. Her energy now seemed to even out.

"Who is it?" She answered with her most elegantly fake hostess voice.

"Hello, it's detective Johnson from the MET Police. Is this Isabella McCarthy? We would like to ask you a few questions." A woman's voice answered. My heart started to beat in my throat, and the police chose today of all days to stop by, right when Isabella was loaded on whatever pills she took. Nevertheless, I kept my cool and nodded at Izzy to meet our uninvited guest while I locked the bedroom door.

"Hi, Detective Johnson. How can we help?" I answered before Isabella's voice gave us both away. I don't think that she suspected anything, these were routine questions, and I didn't want her to come back around for a sniff. The detective pressed for questions for fifteen minutes while Isabella and I answered each of them meticulously. Our performance was flawless, especially when asked if Isabella had seen Mike again after their first encounter at the club. She answered with a solid no and didn't even break a sweat. The fidgety woman I witnessed a few hours ago was gone.

"Like I said, if you remember anything else, please give me a call." She handed Izzy her card and walked herself out the door. Our chest collapsed with a breath of relief, and Izzy made her way to the kitchen for a glass of water. I followed behind her, waiting and took a seat at the island.

"Fuck."

"Shit, shit, shit! Now what?" She paced back and forth while I pondered on our options.

"We just let play out and deal with things as they come. There's no way we could anticipate what they already except that we were all at the club together. The guys took care of his body, and they will never find him-

"We could just kill her too." She blurted out, and my mouth dropped to the floor.

"No, we cannot just kill her! Get your head in the game." But, she knew that killing a detective wasn't going to make the problem go away.

"I have to get some fresh air." Before I could respond, Izzy had run out of the apartment. I hoped she wouldn't do something stupid, and I hung tight for her return.

Chapter Five

Isabella

I needed this high to forget everything wrong with my life and allow my mind to float into nothingness. Every lick and stroke from his tongue pushed me deeper into tranquil bliss. His hands cupped my back while I arched in pleasure, and the scent of his cologne further sizzled my senses. Things got a little too real with the detective's questioning, and I needed an escape. I hadn't spoken to him since that night. I had hoped that he would be home when I rang his doorbell. He was surprised when he saw me but somewhat relieved. I didn't hesitate to come here, but there I was underneath him, soaking up his warmth. The muscles on his arm tensed as he held himself up while he slid in and out of me, sweat glistening our skin. His neck vibrated with the deep grunts and moans, with each one pushing me closer to the edge. I didn't want to regret this. The feeling was too familiar yet so different to being with Ryan. Nathan was genuine. I could feel his yearning to connect with me and indulge in pure intimacy. The kind that makes you go crazy. We had been at him for a while until we both came to a halt of pleasure. My mind was still clouded, but it was a welcomed storm that I didn't want to pass this time. He rolled over and rested his arm on my waist, and I closed my eyes to savour the feeling while it lasted.

"Are you okay?" He traced his hand up to my cheek, and I nodded. I didn't want to talk about how fucked up I was, but I knew that he would eventually start pushing for a deeper conversation. Surprisingly, he rolled out of bed and disappeared out of the room. I took a moment to wonder if he was coming back, but I, being the proud woman I was, decided to take his action as my queue to get dressed and leave. I got out of bed and reached for my clothes. Nathan came back to the bedroom with two small plates. Pastries with intricate icing and toppings. My heart sank.

"You need to stop assuming the worse." I opened my mouth to protest an answer, but he cut me off. "I hadn't heard from you since our date. You're obviously here because you've been having a bad day. This is a moment, don't sabotage it. Here, eat this scrumptious pastry." Without thought, my mouth curved in the biggest smile I've had in a while. He got back into bedplate of pastry in tow, with all of his naked perfection. I guessed this was what ordinary people did.

By the late afternoon, the pills had worn entirely off, and I was surprisingly content to crash in Nathan's bed. I checked my phone here and there to message Frank and keep his mind at peace, but ultimately Nathan was determined to keep me wrapped warmly in his arms, and I was happy to oblige. I eventually woke up to soft kisses being planted on my forehead as my phone simultaneously rang. The screen vibrated with Frank's name, and I rushed out of bed to answer.

"We have a problem." Frank's voice was low and anxious. Shit.

"I'll be there quickly." I said as Nathan's face dropped into a slight frown.

"I'm sorry, I really have to go."

"Okay, let me drive you or at least get you a taxi." His voice was calm. I didn't know what the problem was, but I guessed it was something to do with Mike's disappearance, so I certainly didn't want Nathan involved.

"It's okay, really but thank you. I'll call you soon." I promised.

By the time I arrived at my apartment, Frank was nursing a half tumbler of bourbon in the kitchen. His eyes sank low as he savoured the burn of the elixir. "You are right, Izzy. People always die when you're having fun." He spat. "Hugh has been here looking for his friend and threw some accusations. I don't know how he found your apartment, but it's not looking good with him talking to the detective. "Fuck our lives!" He pinched the bridge of his nose and leaned his head forward. I began to see my best friend unravel. Mine was the choice of a stimulated high, his, was the choice of a liquor-filled downer, and it was my turn to talk him off the ledge.

"You're right, baby, and I'm sorry. I'm so sorry. But you're better than me. You can't drink like this when you're anxious." I took the glass from his hand and crouched in front of him, searching my mind for something to say that would take the edge off his internal panic. "I'm so grateful to have you, Frank. Who do you want me to call to help you in a way that I can't right now?" He didn't have many friendships outside of ours, but I knew he needed the experience I just had with Nathan. My best friend looked straight through me and shrugged. Then I knew who I really needed to call. Lars.

Frank

I don't know what the hell happened to me when Hugh came knocking. For once in my life, I felt powerless and really on edge. I was confused about how he found out where Isabella lived and with him throwing accusations around that were *actually* true. I couldn't make him shut up because that would've caused even more problems for Isabella and me, nor could I run away from the current problem at hand. So I defended us in the best way that fitted, and I don't think it worked. We were well and truly fucked. Then, for the first time in a while, I combined bourbon with my anxiety which eventually unravelled. The entire situation was ridiculous as always, but there was a detective sniffing around this time. When Isabella came back from Nathan's house, I saw that she was just as desolate as I was yet, still motivated to pull me out of the void I had entered. Lars had arrived at her apartment shortly after with Chinese food. Although I couldn't tell him what was happening, he was patient and understanding while walking me to my own place. Once inside my apartment, he served the food and the non-alcoholic beverage from a glowing bottle, which made me cringe thinking about the number of E numbers lingering inside.

"So, what's going on?" He pulled his focus from the plate to my face. I couldn't tell him everything, ever.

"I'm having a bad day. Of course, it's always some type of drama with Izzy. She's my best friend, and I will always support her, but sometimes it gets too much. And today, I discovered I have moderate to severe anxiety." I shrugged as my eyes dropped to the floor.

We continued to eat our food, injecting chatter between bites until I could eventually feel the heavy cloud lifting from my aura. Lars had become a good friend, although there was the added benefit of sleeping together. Lately, we had spent more time talking than touching each other, and it was nice to have conversations with someone other than Isabella.

"It's none of my business, but maybe you spend too much time together." I dropped my fork and glared at him in shock. Not because that he dared to utter those words out loud, but it was that deep down I knew that Isabella and I needed to spend some time apart. We were a platonic couple, and we needed time to breathe. "Or you could start slow and go to counselling? But I'm sure they'll say the same thing." He exhaled an infectious chuckle. I wasn't sure how having space would work for us, and I was concerned now more than ever with the detective enquiring about Mike's disappearance. Counselling sounded like a tangible move. Of course, we couldn't tell the therapist everything, but it could help us find a way to heal our dysfunctionality.

"Counselling is a good idea, actually. Not sure how Izzy will feel about it, but I'll bring it up."

We talked the rest of the afternoon, and I was grateful for Lars. Even though our connection built on the drama of my and Mathew's relationship, it grew deeper since I heard Mathew relocated to the states to live his best life. Now he was a faded memory, and I had bigger fish to fry. With Hugh throwing accusations that could tip the detective on our trail and Isabella's bold idea to kill the detective, I had to ensure I played this situation right and effectively. It's unlikely we would go to prison, but there was a possibility that we could be on the run forever.

Isabella had texted that she had gone to bed just after 9 p.m., and I was honestly grateful to have this time to myself. It was evenings like these that I allowed my mind to frolic in the magic of my lustful past. Although I had grown into a better man, I missed the person I was back when I carelessly partied my nights away and indulged in short-lived romances. Then, life was uncomplicated and square. I saw someone I fancied and fucked them. I saw something I liked, I bought it. Now, everything is calculated to ensure all my tracks were covered. I made sure that I paid every salacious purchase in cash to keep my mundane professional image clean. I mentally vetted my motives before making decisions, and I took it upon myself to keep an eye on Isabella in case she lost control. Sure, she would never want me to think I had to watch out for her, but I hated surprises at this point in my life. My getaway plan was also locked tight in my mind, with all the necessities snug in my grab-bag. Money, gold bars, fake ID cards and passport, a new phone and a map for a remote cottage up north. It would buy me enough time to regroup and work out my next move. Isabella had coached me well. I remember how she handled the situation seamlessly when Ryan was blackmailed and beaten up. The safe in her apartment had everything she needed to survive, and as much as I wanted to put my fate in her hands, ultimately, we would both have to make a decision for ourselves when the time came to survive. I shouldn't be thinking like that, but the truth of this realisation had stirred and lurked in my chest for a while now, and the vibration of that reality was creaking through the surface. Yes, I needed therapy.

The morning after felt somewhat better, so I decided to use the gym before it got busy. After my conversation with Lars, I wondered if counselling was really needed considering the kind of lifestyle Isabella and I lived. How would we even begin to describe our problems without actually telling the truth? Just as I finished my circuit and made my way to the shower, I was summoned to cover an afternoon shift at work. It was unusual for my manager to call me last minute as Stacey, the pretty brunette who usually worked these small private events, loved money as much as I did. Whatever pulled her away from work was, therefore, definitely an emergency. As usual, the first hour on any of my shifts was uneventful, so I made my rounds, chatting to the art buyers and their mistresses, smiling and nodding in agreement until I spotted Hugh lingering at the corner of my eyes. My heart almost stopped, then picked up its beat, my mouth went dry, and my body remained rigid. I was a standing half corpse starring directly at the cunning smile plastered on the familiar face trotting towards me.

"Hello there, Frank." It took everything in me to not kick the shit out of his face.

"Good evening. How are you enjoying the show?" I smiled.

"Quite impressive. I hope to buy a few pieces for a friend of mine." I tensed. He clearly wanted an excuse to cause a scene. "He's one of the cherished few I have left." He was obviously trying to throw me off my guard by bringing this shit up, and I wasn't going to allow it.

"Well, that's great. I hope you find a few that exceeds your expectations. Now, if you'll excuse me." I gave him a curt nod and made my way through the small crowd towards the locker room. There, I loosened my tie and unbuttoned the top of my shirt. *What the hell was I doing?* This despicable creature was having the time of his life when I fucked him to sleep the other night, and he was clearly hung up on the fact that I didn't call him to arrange it again. Then it clicked like the horn of a passing freight train. He had nothing on Isabella and me. He was just using Mike as an excuse to get to me.

"So you're confident this is the case?" Izzy asked while she sautéed vegetables and tossed sauce in the frying pan.

"Yeah, so I think I'll handle that by giving him some attention."

"Sure. Why don't you invite him here for dinner?" She turned around to witness the blank gaze pinned at her. "What? I mean, the best place to hide something is in plain sight, right? And he knows I went home with Mike that night. Obviously, he didn't mention to Hugh that he would come back here, so we have no concrete tie in this. Invite him round to make him feel special by meeting your best friend." She smiled, and the hairs on the back of my neck raised at the way she emphasised the word *special.* Furthermore, it still didn't explain how Hugh found her apartment.

As much as I disliked her proposal, I knew that she was right. It would help keep Hugh close so that I could keep an eye on him. "Fine, I'll call him." She returned to finish cooking dinner.

"I think we should explore counselling." She abruptly stopped in her track and inhaled a deep breath. My heart halted, and I swallowed a lump in my throat. "I mean not because of our mistakes but for the sake of our friendship." She turned to face me.

"What's wrong with our friendship?" For a swift moment, I swore I saw her eyes glisten with moisture.

"I love you, and hear me out before you react." She pressed her lips together. "Lately, I feel that our friendship has shown symptoms of co-dependency. First, I break down and yearn for you and vice versa. Then we both get dragged into a criminal mess." She opened her mouth to protest, but I continued. "Don't get me wrong, I don't regret the shit we've been through together but, don't you think it'll be nice to just have a reprieve?"

The silence lingered between us for a beat before she spoke. "Look, I've been feeling suffocated too. Especially after that prick, Mike. I'm not big on the idea of counselling, but I will do anything to support our friendship."

She attempted a smile as she blinked back a tear. How strange it was to see this turn of event. Isabella, the coldest, most focused, determined, savage person in my world to kill the hardest of men showing vulnerability. I felt honoured to have witnessed this yet concerned. And it was for this precise reason, we needed to talk to someone to help guide us through this phase in our friendship. Sniffing lines, smoking joints and partying our lives away weren't going to fix things. It wasn't even a beautiful plaster to cover the wounds anymore. We were in too deep, and our foundation was getting shaky. I slowly walked towards her and gave her a hug, a simple yet meaningful gesture to let her know that she was still safe with me. I would always be there to wipe her tears, and just like that, she allowed her eyes to weep. A river of suppressed thoughts, frustrations and the remnants of her broken heart flowed onto my t-shirt. I held her tighter as her tiny arms gripped my body closer to her. I knew what she was thinking: we always looked ridiculous in embrace because of our size differences. We stood there until the vegetables burned and the kitchen engulfed in smoke, a beautiful illustration of our chaos.

Isabella

I woke up disoriented and naked. My body was smooth and warm under the thick duvet that weighed on me like the stress of my entire life. The night before was a memory that slowly floated to the surface of my mind as I became more aware of the present. Frank and I had a conversation that wasn't easy, but it was necessary. I loved him, and yes, as much as I didn't want to admit it, we had become or rather, I had become co-dependent on him. I had to cut myself some slack, though, since we both killed someone. Who else could understand me more than he could? "Good morning." Nathan's voice snapped me back into the room. For once, I didn't regret being there. I left Frank sound asleep in my bed, with a note to let him know where I'd gone. I don't know what this thing with Nathan was evolving into, but I do know that I felt amazing waking up in his bed.

"Good morning." I breathed as he climbed back into bed, bringing his kiss to my forehead. At this point, my internal alarm should've been going off. He was too perfect, too honest and too damn handsome, but it didn't, and for as long as I felt like this, I promised myself that I wouldn't sabotage this.

"So, what did you want to do today?"

"I can't stay here all day. I'm sorry, I have to work." It was true. As much as I wanted to stay there and soak up his comfort, I had booked a client in Chelsea, and it was a big enough transaction I never wanted to cancel. Nathan had once inquired about my job, of which I gave the generic answer. Interior design blogger and curator connecting designers and buyers. This was partially true. The blog was a successful anonymous front, but I never had buyers or designers. Although if anyone felt the need to check, my profile would check out fine.
"Okay, well, let's make the most of the time you have right now." He leered, and I returned the gesture. I loved the way his mouth curved into a devious smile. Men. I never ventured into creating friendships with women unless the vibe aligned with mine; however, in my entire

adult life, I have learned that men were the simplest creatures. All I had to do was appeal to their senses, make them feel like they were special, find their weakness and take them for everything they had. Nathan, though, I just wanted him to touch me, and he knew just how and where.

Chapter Six

I couldn't erase the smile on my face when I got back to my apartment. The hours leading up to my exit from Nathan's townhouse were decorated in hesitation. I wanted to soak up his comfort as we lingered in each other's arms after fucking all night. I was exhausted, and for once, I hoped the meeting with my client didn't last longer than I anticipated. He was an investment banker who had booked me for a dinner date. I had confirmed the terms of charges for extra services, knowing that he would propose paying for the extra charge once he saw my curves in a dress. Tonight, however, I was accompanying him as eye candy for his business meeting and rationalised that we would part ways content with the outcome after the deal was made. Frank had gone to the gym, and I wondered if he committed to finding a counsellor for the impending work on our friendship. What a drag our lives had become. After having a shower and getting dressed in my usual work attire, a tailored fitted dress with nude heeled pumps with a killer red lipstick, I ordered a taxi to Chelsea. George and I met through an existing client's recommendation.

My security checks became more vigorous since the John debacle, and my book wasn't always open to new clients. George was legit, and so was his net worth. Securing his clientele for the year ensured that my retirement or getaway account would be solid for another year. I didn't have to worry about my apartment as it was paid for in cash. Everything I owned was replaceable except for the contents in my grab bag planted snuggly in my safe. I lived an extremely comfortable lifestyle, and I extended the privilege to Frank, teaching him the ropes on wealth management and building his accounts offshore in case he needed to disappear. Sure, he didn't divulge his own getaway plan details, but our lives were different now, and we mostly worked for our contingency plans.

The taxi halted, pulling me out of my thoughts. Like many of my clients, George's choice of restaurant was superb. I tipped the taxi driver and entered the foyer, lit with crystal chandeliers, walls decorated with mirrors and gold trims. The host guided me to the table where George greeted me. His mouth curved into a sincere smile as his eyes took in my frame.

"Hello, gorgeous. I hope the journey was okay." He pulled out my chair to accommodate my seat. The table had a bottle of pinot noir and four glasses. "The potential contractors will be arriving shortly." This was his indirect prompt, telling me to play up the charm so he would win. One thing he was yet to know about me was that my team always won. This type of date was strictly business wrapped in a slow seduction. These types of people loved to finesse situations, making deals look way better than what it usually was, and I found that having sex with a man who handed me an envelope of cash, one of the most honest transactions I've ever made. This sort of meeting was constructed on pretence and smiles. However, I would never complain because I had a clear financial goal.

"Yes, the traffic wasn't bad. I'm glad to be here, though." I flashed a demure smile. I was far from shy, although men like George wanted to feel in control. He wanted to be seen with a beautiful good woman on his arm, and that was that.

We made small talk until the other dinner guests arrived, and I immediately stopped dead in my track. My heart raced, and my ears started ringing. I felt dizzy as sweat began to break on my forehead. Shit. I was so careful, but I didn't consider that despite London being a large city, it was also a place where you were likely to bump into people you knew. Especially in the business communities. The guests exchanged greetings and their voices faded in and out of my ears until I felt George's hand on my arm waiting for an answer.

"Hello, it's lovely to meet you." I shook hands with the men that stood in front of me as one of them kept their eyes focused on my face. I kept myself together, but there was no way out of this. Even if it was Nathan sitting opposite me, staring with eyes that could melt ice. I had to give him respect where it was due. He continued to pretend like we didn't know each other, focusing on the business proposals while I smiled and looked pretty, dreading the moment we would all leave. He wasn't stupid, he knew what I was doing there, and quite frankly, I shouldn't have cared about the potential outcome; however, there's something inside me that felt cautious. I felt a fear of loss. The dinner ended well, with everyone satisfied with their roles. Nathan was looking for new investors, and George liked the proposal, negotiated a scrumptious share of the restaurant's profits. I was growing agitated and wanted to leave. George took care of the bill, and we all made our exit.

"I will call you soon, gorgeous." George discreetly said as he kissed my cheeks and slid into his taxi.

I turned around and decided to fish into my handbag for my phone. I wasn't sure what I wanted to do, but I knew that I needed to release the feeling of doom that lurked down my spine. Nathan approached me. He was alone, and we stood looking at each other, doing the awkward dance of silence.

"So, you're with that man?" I rolled my eyes in frustration as I felt the beads of rain on my scalp. Great, just great. "You don't get to roll your eyes here, I asked you to stay with me today, and you said you had to work. Clearly, it was a lie unless-

I waited for him to finish his sentence while my eyes glazed and my monster started to creep from my void. "Say it." I dared him.

"You're a prostitute." He swallowed hard and looked straight through me. It was a look I'd never seen before. He wasn't disgusted or angry. Instead, it was jealousy and confusion.

"An escort. Yes. But it's none of your business what I do. You and I are separate from this." I bit back.

"So, how many have you fucked whilst you were with me, huh?" He barked. "You're right, it's none of my business what you do with your life, but it is when you're fucking my investors."

"Oh fuck you. I don't need your investor. Keep him. I have a long list of clients waiting. And don't act all innocent. I know you've been fucking other women while we've been seeing each other. At least I get paid well." He was stunned and didn't know how to react. Then, the sky sliced open, and a frisson washed over me. My clothes quickly began to soak. I had to get home.

The time it took to arrive home was a blur, and I went straight into a hot shower. I needed to call Frank, but considering the current strain on our friendship, I didn't want to make things worse. I came out of the shower, refreshed, got dressed and ordered myself some food because I barely touched my dinner, then poured myself a tumbler of bourbon. It had been a while since I indulged in my favourite tiple, and it was time to unleash my inner demons. As I sipped and nursed the slow burn in my throat, I came to terms with the fact that this is who I really was. A beautiful ball of chaos. Who was I fooling, or what the hell was I trying to prove by trying to be good. All the nonsense about mending a broken heart, trying to live a semi-normal life. It wasn't who I was. I thrived in chaos and drama. The passion and lustful adventures of life are what made me feel alive. I guess a part of me knew that I was trying to live my life for Frank. I felt guilty for dragging him down with me. When my food was delivered, I rode a pleasant buzz that elevated my tastebuds. I scoffed the pasta quickly and tossed the containers in the bin. Washed my hands and slipped my body into a pair of jeans and a cashmere jumper. I pulled my hair in a high ponytail, slapped on some red lipstick and a pair of black heels. It was officially summer, but the night's air was crisp. I grabbed my bag, keys and phone to make my way out of the door, where Nathan's finger was pointed at the doorbell. Here we go.

"You know you've never invited me to your house, and now I know why." My trigger alarm should've gone off, but I wasn't worried about Nathan.

"If you're here for an argument, I'm not interested. I'm going out." He backed away and pinched the bridge of his nose.

"Let's talk. That's all I want. Please." The truth was, I didn't know where I was going. Maybe a bar or a spa, but it wouldn't have been better than being with him, so I let him in.

"Wow, you have excellent taste. Did you decorate yourself?" He said as he walked towards the living room.

"Yep. Drink?" He nodded. I poured us both some bourbon and stood in the kitchen close enough to the knives in case he had ulterior motives. Call me crazy, but my guard was always up after Mike's shenanigans. We sipped our drinks quietly.

"I didn't plan to not tell you about my job, and I'm not apologising for anything."

"A job is a job. We all have to find ways to empower ourselves. I respect you, but I can't share you." I was taken aback. Most men would've disengaged and ran a mile. The fact that he respected me mildly stroked my ego. Nonetheless, this was now a complicated situation. I didn't want him asking around about me because then I would have to kill him. I couldn't risk myself or Frank going to prison. Nathan would be nothing but collateral damage.

"Why are you here then? I won't stop doing what I do. You're wasting your time." I raised my brows. Truthfully, I was enjoying this. He was lingering between desire, lust and logic. Logically, he knew that this was a dead-end, that he should run away while he still could, but his lustful desire wouldn't let him. He had a taste of me, and he couldn't let it go. That's the battle men went through once they've tasted good pussy. And I knew exactly what was coming.

"I'm here because-

He grabbed his hair and paced to the living room.

"I fucking love you!" Well, that was certainly unexpected. Love, really? We've been having a good time, but I know that I definitely didn't love him. Not when my heart still belonged to someone else. And what was I supposed to say to that? "Yes, it's too soon, and god knows you're a mess." Me? A mess? "I've fallen in love with you, and that's that. But I can't share you." Well, what a predicament for him.

"I can't change who I am for you." He slowly walked towards me until his chest touched mine, our breaths tangled with the kiss of death. My heart raced, and I loved how he made me feel. I had nothing to lose but myself. And every time I felt this way, I ended up in a place so deep that I could barely pull myself out. I would move mountains for this feeling, even killed for this feeling, and I was okay with that.

"Then tell me to leave." He was insane, but I was already on the ledge. Standing on the brink of a fall without a life jacket because that's how I lived my life. Our lips touched, and his warmth was intoxicating. Our kiss grew deeper, more challenging, until my hand was wrapped around his throat, showing him that I was the boss of my life. So there we were, in my kitchen with our tongues entangled while we undressed each other until I was left in nothing but my heels, bent over the island with my legs spread. He pressed into me, and I pushed out a light gasp. He was hard, and I welcomed him. My lips glistened with moisture as I let him enter me with ease, our moans matching intones. "You don't want me to leave, baby." He whispered in between my moans as he pumped harder and faster into me. I was on the brink of ecstasy, swimming in the fantasy of us lost in a world where passion came before the consciousness of complications of a broken heart and murder. Suddenly a primal groan pulled me from thoughts. My legs shook towards their weakness, and I felt complete as he lost himself inside his orgasm. For sure, this was way better than whatever I thought I was going to do that night.

"Now what?" He whispered while his hand stroked my hair, and the other brought his drink to his lips.

"You said you didn't want to share me, so this is the end, I guess." I knew this conversation was coming, and as much as I wanted to enjoy his warmth a little longer, I knew that it was better we ended things now before he got hurt too. We didn't have to say anything else as we simmered on the sofa for a while. Then, when the right moment arrived, he stood up and left. I fell asleep with my void wide open, missing Frank.

Frank

The waiting room was white and had green plants in pretty much every corner. Isabella was unusually quiet, but I couldn't blame her since there were a million other things that we both would rather be doing on a Friday afternoon. I firmly believed that this was a healthy step for our friendship, and if it didn't work out, at least we both tried. We were the only people in the waiting room, and I was glad. I shouldn't care what others thought of me, but the stigma of men going to therapy still runs deep, and one judgement wouldn't really help my already anxious mind. Just as I contemplated pulling out my phone to play a game for distraction, our names were called. The counsellor was a man in his mid-fifties. I thought it would be a good idea to choose someone that neither of us would be attracted to. However, where Izzy was concerned, It was difficult for men to stay away from her.

"Hello, I'm doctor Chris. How can I help you today, Christophe?" He said with indifference.

"Well, we've been struggling with some co-dependency issues in our friendship." I paused for his response, but he just wrote some notes, gesturing for me to continue. "Lately, it seems that whenever something goes wrong in both of our lives, we end up dragging each other in the drama. And they're usually quite big, the type that takes away a good night's sleep." Izzy shot me a look, but she stayed quiet.

"Well, talking it out and getting some help is a step in the right direction. And Juliana, what would you like to add?" Of all the names she could've chosen, she decided to use Juliana. But I supposed it fitted the façade we were trying to pull here. Christophe and Juliana were innocent.

Isabella paused before speaking. "He's right. Lately, we have been too dependent on each other, but I don't trust too many people, and he is my best friend." Dr. Chris smiled empathetically as Izzy continued. "Things have been unravelling, and Christophe arrives at the wrong time, I guess." Well, that wasn't always true, but at least she was honest. Dr. Chris continued to listen and take notes while we took turns speaking on our internal dilemmas. It was a mildly positive experience, but when the session time ran out, I realised that as much as I wanted to perhaps blame Izzy for this co-dependency issue that Lars worked in my head, I was the one that needed to address something inside. Isabella knew who she was, ruthless and honest. This, however, was new to me. Yes, I had gotten into a bit of trouble before that prompted my acquaintance with the guys, but I had never murdered someone. I had never been in the middle of blackmail and games. I was carrying a subconscious fear that I didn't even know I had and guilt that I thought I was beginning to release. Shit. I needed counselling alone.

"So you're telling me that we wasted a Friday afternoon because you didn't know that you needed counselling sessions alone?" Izzy snarled at me as we sat at a bar in

Convent Garden, the night's light reflecting her dark eyes.

"I'm not sorry that we went. It brought things into perspective. You know who you are, and I'm just starting to come to terms with who I've become." I sipped my drink. "Oh, and Juliana? Fucking really?" I chuckled, and she was instantly infected to join in.

"I know. It was the only name I could think of." We both laughed so hard that the other patrons glanced at us with mild annoyance. "Now what?" She stared straight into my soul, and I saw the familiar devilish twinkle in her eyes.

Chapter Seven

Frank

It was 11 p.m. when Izzy and I entered *Bar Hugh* for the first time in ages. Not a lot had changed except for the new gorgeous bartenders, Lars included, who was gracious to book us a booth at the last minute. We planned on having some fun like the good old days. Besides, our birthdays were only a few days away, and we may as well get the celebration started. Our booth had the best view, showcasing the packed bar and more people coming in with each minute that went by. It was a Friday night full of possibilities. Izzy had excused herself for the ladies, and I spotted eyes tracing her frame as she made her way back to our booth. She would turn heads even in skinny jeans, simple heels and a shirt. I'm sure men wanted to approach her but were always intimidated by my presence. First, because I was big enough to not be fucked with. Second, because they thought I was her boyfriend or overprotective brother. This was plausible since we looked similar, except she was feminine, pretty with long hair. I smiled to myself.

"I would go with the overprotective brother." Izzy spat with a chuckle. Of course, we knew each other so well that she knew exactly what I was thinking, but mostly we had done this routine so many times since we first met.

"Let the games begin." We clinked our glasses and sipped our drinks as the jittery high from the white lines we inhaled before leaving the other bar crept to our brains. We danced. Our hearts pounded to the beat of the music until we eventually got separated. At first, I wasn't worried since Izzy was a grown woman I didn't have to babysit. I ventured to the bathroom to freshen up, leaving her to her own devices. But when I came back to the booth, she was nowhere to be found.

"Have you seen Isabella?" I asked Lars, who shook his head.

"Maybe she went outside for some air?" I nodded and made my way out of the bar, where I found her pacing up and down the pavement with her arm out. Suddenly a taxi stopped.

"What the fuck is going on?" She shot me a look of fire that made my blood run cold. There was only one thing that grabbed my full attention at this point in my life. It was Isabella's anger.

"You! You fucking talk to Ryan!" She growled. How the hell did she even know that. "He called your phone while you were in the toilet, you prick!" She answered as though reading my mind. Shit. "How could you do this after everything we've been through." My heart raced when her tears flowed down her cheeks and onto the ground. It was like we were standing on a piece of bread that got soggy with each drop that would eventually break, and we would fall to be lost in the darkness forever.

"He was checking to see if you're okay, that's all. I swear."

"Yet, you didn't have the balls to tell me. You let me go on and on about him." I stepped towards her to stop her from getting into the taxi, but she was quick. Just like that, our Friday night descended into a muddy mess.

I went back inside to find Lars, then changed my mind since I didn't want to hear his consulting sermons and 'I told you so'. This time it was definitely on me for fucking up. I should've told Izzy about my contact with Ryan, but part of me didn't even think she would find out. It wasn't malicious, and I thought I was doing what was best for her, but subconsciously I was a little jealous. I wanted her to be happy, but regardless of how fucked up our lives were, I wanted a romantic partner to care about me too. Yes, I messed up with Mathew, and I would probably never change. Nonetheless, it was nice to see Ryan still passionate about her. Nathan was nice, but there was no way he would cope with Izzy the way Ryan did. They were a force together. And I wanted my own soldier to fight for me too. I should've gone home after we fought, but I didn't.

"So what happened after she left, Frank?" I was sitting in Dr. Chris' office with bated breath, trying to make sense of the thoughts circling in my head. Nothing new happened the night before. I left *Bar Hugh* with a random and fucked my pain away.

"I went home with a random guy." I pinched the bridge of my nose. "I didn't even have fun. I just did what was familiar to numb my emotions." Dr. Chris listened intently as he prompted me to speak. It felt nice to just talk out loud. Of course, I had no intentions to divulge all the murdering details, but with each word I uttered, I felt the noose around my neck relax.

"You need to reach deeper, Frank. We often become the characters we portray in adulthood because of a trauma that happened to us in childhood. And that trauma is usually a repressed memory, so painful that we bury it deep as though it never happened. But for you to heal in the present for an optimistic future, you need to allow yourself to visit your past and address that trauma to eventually let it go." He proceeded to write some notes. "Are you having trouble sleeping, having panic attacks or experiencing episodes of depression?" This question caught me off guard. I wasn't sure why he asked this and wondered if my internal pain was that obvious.

"Last week, I had a panic attack for the first time." I kept my answer vague in case it was a test to have me bound to an insane asylum. Although the thought of being in a ward with free pills, silence and nothing but a bed sounded appealing to me at that moment.

"Did you self-medicate?" He looked at me, scanning for the truth. "This is a safe space for you." I didn't believe I was safe anywhere. The word triggered my survival instinct.

"No, I didn't self-medicate." Dr. Chris paused for a moment and started scribbling something down on a piece of paper, tore it from the book and handed it to me. Instructions for breathing techniques.
He handed me a black notebook. "I strongly encourage you to start journaling every day. Start with how you feel every morning and night. Then I want you to write a list of situations where you felt hurt in your childhood. We'll discuss it further in our next session." Just like that, I was dismissed. Dr. Chris wasn't a counsellor who held patients hands and stroked their hair. Nevertheless, he got results, and the recommendations were excellent for that alone.

I left his office trying to not judge myself for agreeing to journal. I had never done that in my life, and the more I spoke with Dr. Chris, the more clarity I gained for my life. The idea of digging deep to bring up suppressed trauma to heal was scarier than Isabella's anger. Nonetheless, It had to be done. It was a mild Saturday afternoon, and I was grateful that I had the funds to pay for the emergency session. It wasn't cheap. On the way home, I stopped by our favourite bakery and bought some sweet pastries and gooey hot chocolates as an apology for Izzy. We hadn't spoken since the night before, and I didn't attempt to contact her. I knew it was best to let her cool down with some space. At this point, though, I knew that she had enough space. It was time for me to break the ice and accept whatever insults she would serve. Surprisingly, I was much calmer since my session with Dr. Chris.

"Izzy, stop being a brat and open the door. You also gave me a key." I spoke through the door. Silence. "I know you're in there. I can hear you angry breathing." Still nothing. "I have pastries and hot chocolate from your favourite bakery." A brief pause and the door opened. I gave her a gentle smile as I entered. "They're freshly baked too." We walked to the living room, where she sat and shuffled a book on the other side of the sofa.

We ate our pastries in silence, broken by the occasional sips of our beverage. She hadn't forgiven me because I knew the extent of her stubbornness, and I was okay with that. "I'm sorry, Izzy. I honestly wasn't even thinking. I just assumed you would be alright regardless and didn't consider that it would trigger you. And I wasn't talking to Ryan like we were friends. It's usually a text every couple of weeks confirming you were okay. Calls were rare, and there were no long conversations."

"It's not the first time you kept something from me, Frank. You remember what happened with John." Wow, of all the insults, I couldn't believe that she threw that in my face. The situation with John was different. He had us both under his thumb deep in his game. He blackmailed me. And I was definitely a different person back then.

"That was different. This wasn't malicious. It was ensuring that you were okay." My anger simmered. I wanted to grab the pastry from her hand and get the fuck home. "Let's not turn this into something it isn't. You're pissed, fine. But don't throw this John shit in my face, especially when we both had a part to play in this." I could've dragged her to filth with my petty words, but I refrained from making things worse.

"Oh yeah, I know it's all my fault. Say it! That's your real problem. Resentment. You could've saved us both that stupid fucking trip to Dr. Chris if you just admitted it. You resent me and our friendship." I really didn't want to go there with her, but she pushed for a fight.

"Fine. Since that day, I found Andrew's body in your living room. We've been a mess. You didn't even have the courtesy to stop and think about how it would affect my life when you called me that morning. I warned you many times, but you had to go fuck around with these grown men. Now, look at us! Look at you and look at me. I can barely sleep, and you can't even move on from the man you weren't even supposed to have. You fucked his brother, then killed him. Amongst other things you got me involved in." My chest raised heavily as my breath thickened with anger.

"And you've become needy since you cheated on Mathew. Don't act all innocent like I forced you to do anything. Yes, at some point, I called you since you're the only person I trust, but you get off on the chaos too. You cheated on Mathew when you had something great going for you. You got a kick out of playing detective the past few months, so spare me the moral high ground. So go and see Dr. Chris, but tell him that you are your own problem. Don't blame it on our friendship. Blame yourself." She spat. The words should've hurt, but it was the truth that triggered my need to accept myself.

We stood in the middle of her living room, staring at each other. Lioness versus angry wild bull. A disaster waited to unfold until she broke our gaze and walked to the kitchen, and poured herself some juice.

"Gosh, you make me so fucking crazy." She shouted.

"Right back at you, baby." I said playfully with a chuckle that I knew would make her madder that she had no choice but to smile back. I approached her with my arms wide open, and she accepted my embrace. We were both crazy. Hers floated on the surface while mine lurked in a void. "Dr. Chris gave me a journal to heal my subconscious wounds." I laughed. Not because I thought it was a joke, it's because I never saw myself in this position in life.

"Good. I journal every day too." She whispered in my chest.

"Well, I didn't know that. Now we have one more thing in common.'

We hung out at her apartment for a while before I headed home.

"Isabella knows we're talking. You need to stop fucking around and make up your mind. You're either with her, or you're not." I scowled through gritted teeth as the man on the other side of the line sighed. "What's happened in the past is in the past. You can't keep living like this." I continued. "I mean it Ryan, consider this our last phone call. We have to move forward." I hung up before he had a chance to respond. I didn't want to get into a conversation with him. We weren't friends. And I didn't want to cause any more pain to Isabella.

My mind was surprisingly clear for a Saturday night. Usually, I'd be floating high as I inhaled clouds of smoke, but after our earlier fight, I just wanted to focus on the homework Dr. Chris assigned. I stared at the notebook for a while as I calculated how to approach journaling. Eventually, I closed my eyes and let my hand move the pen. When I was done, my eyes gazed down at the words that spilt on multiple pages. Ten of them, to be precise. Not bad. I decided to reward myself with a little high, but as I approached the cabinet for my secret stash of self-medication, my chest felt heavy, and a cloud of darkness washed over me. Fuck. Tears, literal tears started pouring out of my eyes, and the sobs that came from the pit of my stomach knocked me off my feet. *What the hell was going on?* A few minutes later, I felt myself lying on my bedroom floor, eyes puffy and my skin prickling with heat. I should've felt embarrassed, but I knew deep down that I needed this, and I was glad that it happened in the privacy of my own home. Ten minutes later, I decided to order some pasta for dinner. Again, I felt ten pounds lighter as my belly roared with hunger. The food eventually arrived, and I found myself enjoying my own company for the first time in a long while. Although I still stuck to my self-medicating reward, there was no need to pretend to be happy and high. I ate my dinner in peace while I enjoyed the tranquilising calm of the pills.

Chapter Eight

Isabella

I woke up at 3 a.m. to the disruptive sound of my doorbell. I grabbed my baseball bat and ensured my safe was locked before I treaded lightly towards the front door. I knew who it was since I had integrated a camera with my doorbell. Nonetheless, I couldn't place my trust in anyone since Mike's violation. I opened the door and saw his brows furrowed with confusion that I mirrored.

"I can't stop thinking about you." Here we go. "I tried, but I need to be near you." They always did. Nathan no longer had a seat in my mind. We said all that we had to that night he left. And I didn't think I would see him again. And there he was.

"It's 3 o'clock in the morning. You couldn't call beforehand or wait for a decent time?" I smiled, not quite knowing if I wanted to invite him inside or make him sweat a little. The early autumn air was settling as the breeze blew into the open window from the landing. I didn't want to stand there any longer, so I invited him in.

We didn't do much talking when the door shut. I climbed back into bed and waited to see his next move. "Wow, you're paranoid." He said as his eyes met my baseball bat that rested in the corner of my bedroom. We both soaked in silence as I felt no need to justify my actions to anyone in my own home. Finally, satisfied that I wasn't giving anything away, he undressed down to his boxers and climbed into bed next to me.

"There's a spare toothbrush in the bathroom cupboard. Use it." I commanded. He obeyed and got back into bed.

We slipped into a lull where I drifted into a realm of ancestral visitation.

"Mother, father!" I ran into their welcoming embrace. There were no other words to describe the feeling except pure comfort and safety. The safety I've craved my entire adult life. Here, we sat in serenity to talk about life and its achievements. Here, I let my doubts and fear boil on the surface, knowing that my parents would always have words of wisdom that would help me get through any situation. This was a place of truths. Where the resilient mask I glued on my character and face peeled off, exposing my raw flesh, where I could showcase the fragmented pieces of my heart without the fear of judgement. I was allowed to cry through my sorrows and express happiness like a child in this place. Since my parents died, something inside me shifted as though I knew that I was meant to live a broken life. It was knowledge that sparked into manifestation by the disastrous events of my childhood. I couldn't express enough that I missed them every day. Sometimes I sat on the balcony in the dark, looked up at the stars wondered what my life would be like if I still had a solid family unit. I wondered about life after death, how many lifetimes it would take until I saw them again. I thought about whether they would approve of my friendship with Frank. Would I have ever met Frank if they were still with me? Perhaps I would've been sent to an elite university where I would've met him during my young adult rebellion anyway. It didn't matter, though, because the fact was

that they were dead. And there we were, smiling at each other as we sat at our dining table while the staff rallied around us, ensuring I had the best birthday ever. "We love you so much, Izzy." Both my parents said as they began to fade into nothing. The room spun into a tornado of mist, and eventually, there was nothing but darkness and sadness. I sat on the floor and crouched my head in between my legs, cradling my sadness. Tears, thick and salty, cascaded down my cheeks. Then, I was rewarded with the wish I sometimes asked the gods. My heart stopped.

Big hands caressed my shoulders as I stirred into reality, my mind taking forever to catch up with my surrounding. "Hey, you were crying and shouting in your sleep. It must've been a terrible dream. Want to talk about it?" Nathan looked into my eyes, but the door to my soul was already shut and locked. I climbed off the bed and went into the bathroom to wash my face and brush my teeth. The tiny gold clock on the counter confirmed 7 a.m., and I wanted to kick myself for waking up this early on a Sunday. The only thing that could steer my day into the light now was a long run in the park. I walked back into the bedroom to put on my running kit. Nathan reclined on the bed, scrolling through his phone.

"I'm going for a run." I coldly announced and left before he had a chance to respond. The past few weeks had been a blur. One minute it was spring, and now the brown leaves crunched under my feet, marking the transition of autumn. Although, the sky was still bright. Not that I was ever afraid of being attacked. The park began to fill up with other runners and dog walkers, most of them probably rudely awakened by bad dreams too.

Zoning out, I focused solely on my breath running until my lungs and legs ached.

I arrived home to find the coffee table filled with breakfast stuff. Homemade pastries, eggs, veggie sausages, juice and a pot of tea. I would be lying if I wasn't turned on by the fuss Nathan had made, but I couldn't show him that and let him off the hook easy. He couldn't think that he could end things and come back into my life whenever he felt like it. I quickly showered and dressed into some casual loungewear. My stomach rumbled when I smelled the fresh pastries.

"I hope you don't mind me using the kitchen. It's quite spectacular. I couldn't help myself." He smiled as I sipped some juice and proceeded to bite into the pastries.

"Not at all. This is delicious." The compliment made him giddy. We finished breakfast and talked about mundane subjects before Nathan prodded his questions.

"So, what was your dream about?" He waited patiently as I debated whether to confess or not. At this point, I wanted to vocalise it, and since I didn't want to bother Frank on his mini R&R, I decided to come clean.

"My parents. They died when I was a teenager." I circled my thumb on the rim mug in my hand.

"I'm sorry to hear that. Were you close with them." I nodded.

"It wasn't a bad dream. At least it didn't feel like it until I was on the brink of waking up." He nodded. I didn't want to go deeper into this conversation. There were so many questions circling in his head, and each one led to an answer that he couldn't handle. Nathan was clean and legit. I had the guys do a background check on him and his family. There was nothing that suggested he was in any kind of criminal activity. I wanted him to stay that way. Then there were questions about my profession. I wouldn't give up this part of myself for anyone.

"I just wanted to see you. I've missed you." It had only been a few days, but I smiled gently at him, not having the heart to confess that I had moved on rather quickly.

"Okay, but now what?"

"I want to have a relationship with you." I opened my mouth to protest, but he continued. "I know, you're never giving up your job. I get it. I'm not saying we become a couple. More like friends who have sex." I pondered his words for a moment. I had never been in a friend with benefits situation. It could complicate things, or it could be the best balance ever. Someone to talk to and have fun with without fully committing.

"Fine. But there'll be no mention of my work, and you will treat me as a friend, not your escort."

"Okay. I just want to be a part of your life." This man was absurd. The entire situation was crazy, but it felt right, quite comfortable.

We spent the rest of the morning chatting about his work and our workout routines. Eventually, we ended up with our bodies entwined in my bed. That was where I felt the most at peace for a short while until it was time to go about our day.

"Stay in bed with me." He lightly resisted when I shuffled for my exit.

"All day?"

"Yes, all day. We can watch TV, drink some wine, order food. Come on, how often do you get the opportunity to do that?" He wasn't wrong. Lately, I had been making myself busy obsessing over ledgers and the Mike situation. It would've been nice to indulge for a while longer. So I did.

It was just after 7 p.m. when my phone started ringing constantly. I had crashed in Nathan's nook since we finished streaming a series and had dinner. He was fast asleep when the phone rang for the third time.

"I'm coming up. Detective Johnson just paid me a visit." Then, suddenly, the bubble of indulgence crumbled around me, and the walls closed in. It was time to put my game face on.

"Nathan, get up. My friend's coming over. You have to leave." I shuffled out of bed and turned on the lights to force him awake. He hesitated but proceeded to climb out of bed and got dressed when he saw that I wasn't joking.

"I guess I'll see you soon then." He hissed. There's no doubt that he was pissed, but I didn't have the faculty to deal with his attitude when I had more pressing matters to attend to. He exited my apartment and slammed the door to convey his annoyance like a child. Shortly after, Frank arrived.

"Loverboy looked pissed. Sorry to disturb you, but this is urgent." I didn't care if Nathan was pissed because my fighting instinct was in overdrive.

"He'll live. So tell me everything." I announced as I poured us both a glass of wine.

"At first, I thought she would arrest me, considering it's a Sunday. I thought someone like her would only make a house call on a weekend if it was an emergency. But she started acting weird. Making subliminal threats like she knew what we did to Mike. Her demeanour was quite aggressive in a sharky way."

"Shit. I think it may be time to get our getaway plans in motion. We can't sit here and wait for her to come with her grubby handcuffs. How did she even know where you live? We met her here." My mind was spinning.

"Who cares? She's exhibited crook behaviour. Either someone tipped her off, or she's trying to scare us into blackmail. And we've played this game before and won. We can do it again. I had the guys tap into the security cameras to track her car registration. Whatever she's up to, we'll know by tomorrow morning." It was the wrong time to think about it, but I couldn't smile at how diligent

Frank was. He was on his feet, ready to push back and find a solution. This was the man I trusted with my life.

We stayed up late, coming up with ideas for approaching the situation. This was an unusual occurrence, unlike the events of the past. This time, a detective was involved, and we had to be extremely careful.

Frank fell asleep with his hands clutched around his phone. We woke up at 6 a.m., ready to face the day. The breakfast routine that was once an exciting ritual was now lacklustre. Still, it was a positive sign as our robotic moves pulled our focus on the matter at hand. Life was now on pause until this was resolved. Just as I poured myself a glass of orange juice, Frank's phone rang.

"Yep, okay, hmm hmm. Got it." He took a sip of his coffee after hanging up. "They have her address, but there are cameras everywhere. It'll take another hour for them to hack in and give us a window for a little snoop." I stared at him wide-eyed. When did he become so game? It's as if he had turned into me. "I've learned from the best. You have your nerve, and I have mine." He smiled.

We waited for the go-ahead from the guys to make our move. It wasn't until 9 a.m. when they confirmed it was okay to go. The plan was to get inside the detective's house through the back gate where they had frozen the cameras. One of the guys had done a quick scan of the area and property. Lucky for us, she lived in a detached house, and as long as we were careful, nobody should be able to spot us going in. Getting into the house was tricky considering she would have security alarms activated, which is where the guys' trusted device that jammed the signals and suppressed the network came in handy. The system won't trip, and the monitoring company wouldn't be alerted. Fun. Once inside, we had approximately fifteen minutes to get what we needed, which would be a challenge since I had no clue what exactly we were looking for except for anything that stood out for attention. By 9.30 a.m., our white van parked at the back of the property. It was surreal to actually experience a glimpse of a day in 'The Guys' life. I didn't know their names as they were rightfully cautious. They looked like ordinary men in fitted shirts and chinos to the outside world. Some wore glasses, while others had impeccable haircuts. However, we knew that they weren't the type to take anything lightly. You called, they delivered, no questions asked about the situations but rest assured they ran a lucrative business. If you didn't pay up, they knew how to tie up loose ends and how to successfully get rid of a body. They weren't the types for small talk either. So as Frank and I sat in the refurbished van decorated with futuristic screens and devices, I didn't even know existed enjoying the comfortable seats (like the inside of a fancy tour bus), I found myself avoiding eye contact and pressing my lips together in an attempt to refrain from saying the wrong thing.

Cameras frozen, we made our way through the back gate that the guys unlocked by hacking the code, likewise with the backdoor that led the entrance to the kitchen. The house itself was pretty on the outside, but the inside indicated Detective Johnson's personality. She was a slob. Dirty plates crusted with old food littered her sink and counter. Empty wine glasses stained with red tannings were dotted around the kitchen. Clearly, she was a workaholic, but I had to wonder why she couldn't just get a housekeeper, as well as resist a chuckle when I took a glance at Frank's reaction. So far, nothing stood out except for her dirty kitchen. We proceeded down the hallway to the dining room filled with laundry and empty bottles of alcohol. "Oh god, it gets worse," I muttered to Frank, who was well out of his element. The living room was somewhat better, although it was definitely lived in. I didn't want us lingering there for longer than necessary, so I prodded Frank upstairs where the thick smell of stale harassed our nostrils. She hadn't opened a window since she moved in, it seemed, nor had she vacuumed the carpets. We quickly scanned each room, starting with the main bedroom. The bed was undone, and more clothes littered the floor. I was sincerely hoping that she didn't have a pet, but I halted when I saw movements under the pile of garments draped on the floor. A kitten peeked out, poor creature. He was tiny, and it mewed in distress. Being the gentle giant he was, Frank leapt to the kitten and swept it in his arms. Yep, we had a new addition to the family. The bathroom was the worse with what I assumed was white tiles, which were crusted in mould and grime. Our feet quickly shuffled back onto the landing, kitten in tow. Finally, a door left ajar beckoned us into her home office. We froze in our tracks when we saw the wall covered with photos, diagrams, bold writing in red markers and hundreds of pages with multiple investigations. The desk was covered in post-it notes and reminders.

Jax- visit Tuesday/ Hide evidence.

Jane- Visit Thursday/ lock door.

Promotion- Present investigation link/ John + Andrew.

Clear path for the wolf

"What the fuck. She's onto us, Izzy." Frank shook his head as he pinched his eyes shut. I took a breath, as deep as I could without vomiting from disgust and looked slowly at the wall.

"No, not just us. She's been at this for a while like a dog with a bone. My guess is she's dying for the alpha position and a promotion." I pointed to the notes on the desk. "Look. See, she's in debt or mentally unstable" There was no way someone would live like this for nothing. Judging by the state of her house, my instincts suggested she was in some kind of trouble. Perhaps she borrowed money from the wrong people to feed an addiction. Frank wasn't convinced.

"What are you doing?" He coaxed as I slid a pin out of my hair and unlocked the desk drawer. I searched through the papers and thick books until one caught my eyes. A black notebook, similar to Andrew's.

"See, bank statements. She's overdrawn." I flipped the plastic sleeves, and some loose pages fell out. "Mortgage repayments, overdue. She's in the red, Frank." I continued to look through the papers. "Large cash withdrawals fortnightly like she's on a schedule. She's in deep trouble, so she needs to make something out of anything to pass as a solid investigation for that promotion. Her connection probably needs her in the alpha seat at this job so she can clear their tracks. And looking at these notes, it looks like her colleagues don't know what this is. I think we have a chance here." Frank pondered on my words and quickly fished for his phone to take pictures of everything on the wall and the desk. I folded everything as they were and locked it back in place. I checked the time, and we quickly made our exit by slipping out the backdoor and out of the gate. Locking it as it was.

When we entered the van, the guys were busy executing another mission. Inside, I admired their work ethic and dedication to making money. Frank and I slipped off our gloves and protective shoe coverings, slipping them in a disposal bin as instructed as we drove off. When we were a few miles down the road, I searched my mind for a way out of this shit. I was good at this, especially when under pressure. Detective or not, she wasn't going to bother myself or Frank ever again. The kitten stirred slowly on my lap and lightly purred itself back to sleep. I guess it was relieved to be out of that shithole of a home. I lightly patted its head when I noticed one of the guys looking at me with a grin. He reached behind the seat and pulled out a small bag.

"It needs food and milk." I froze with apprehension when I heard his accent. He sounded Russian. There were five of them, and I had only spoken to two so far. The other three were silent deterrents for trouble. They did the heavy lifting while the others specialised in hacking and organising. The Russian laughed when he saw the confusion on my face. He obviously did this often, rescuing animals during criminal activities. Why else would he have a bag of kitty food? "Take it. I'll add it to your tab." He exposed a wide grin.

"Thanks." I quickly took the bag and prayed we got back to my apartment soon to escape the palpable awkwardness. It's not that he was intentionally being awkward. The man was nice in body and face; however, I didn't know them very well, and I was adamant about maintaining the line of boundaries to avoid personal involvement. This was strictly business. We weren't here to make friends.

My chest collapsed with relief when the van stopped outside my apartment. I handed the lead a roll of notes and got the hell out of there, forcing Frank to catch up.

"Where's the fire?" Frank chuckled. "He liked you. He's never spoken out around me before." He continued to tease a laugh.

"Oh, piss off Frank." I giggled as we walked into my living room, where I sat the little kitty on the sofa while I prepped its bowls. Minutes later, the kitten food and milk were served. The poor fluff ball gobbled it up like it hadn't eaten in days. "Is it male or female?" Frank shrugged, and we found ourselves online searching *How to tell if a kitten is male or female?*

Soon enough, we determined that it was a male. Frank was ecstatic, and it was bizarre to experience us stepping into caregiver roles. One thing we were sure of was that the kitten was staying with me. The Russian had conveniently scanned him for a microchip despite reassuring us that it was unlikely he had one, but it was always better to be sure. And we were happy that the kitten came with a clean slate.

"What should we name it?" Frank pondered for a moment.

"Hmmm, how about Jules?" It was settled. We officially welcomed Jules into our dysfunctional family.

"I love it."

Chapter Nine

Isabella

We spent the rest of the day watching Jules settling in his new home while I mentally planned our next move. I decided it was time to blindside Detective Johnson somewhere she'd least expected me. After all, she did invite herself to Frank's apartment, and I deemed it was time for us to return the favour. Now that we had an idea of the games the detective was possibly playing, it was time to make a move. The plan was to make our presence known when she was busy indulging in her after work liquor. It was a Monday. We figured she'd be dying to get home to her beloved habits. I wondered if she would notice that Jules was missing.

We made our way back to her house in the same van from our earlier visit, only this time, I had contingency strategies to ensure our freedom. I kept most of the details from Frank since I didn't want him to get edgy again, he was doing great, but I knew that we all had our limits. All I asked for was his trust.

In the van, the Russian seemed more comfortable at this point, and I think Frank was right. He did like me. Regardless, my head was in the game. Our freedom was on the line. I had to focus. The same earlier routine was performed, cameras frozen, and alarms deactivated. We slipped through the back door into the dark kitchen. A faint glow seeped inside from the living room. I halted to listen, but she wasn't there. I left Frank to keep a lookout while I grabbed a decanter of whiskey, took a swig and ventured upstairs searching for my prey. She was immersed in her grime crusted bath. My face cringed at the thought of anyone actually enjoying that space. I slowly entered to interrupt her bath of horrors, leaving her shocked. She was quick to jump out of the water but not as quick as I pushed her against the cold tiles and forced my hand on her mouth. Her resistance was strong, but my technic was stronger.

"You picked the wrong person to intimidate." I spat each word with venom. "Don't worry, all the cameras and alarms are disabled. You and I are gonna have a chat." I sunk a syringe into her arm before she tried to protest. A time-released solution of Vicodin and Diazepam. Within seconds her body relaxed. She was lucid enough to grasp what was occurring but not enough to fight. I propped her out of the bath, draped her body in a musty bathrobe then moved to her home office. I checked the time to see that we had twenty minutes to get all the answers we sought.

"Who are you working with?" She rolled her eyes to glare at the wall. "I won't ask you again."

"The big bad wolf." She attempted a laugh. "What are you going to do, kill me? You are way down the rabbit hole, and it gets deeper."

"And I supposed you're close to tying up your investigation for that promotion?"

"Well, not everyone can afford expensive habits. Plus, it'll be nice for the wolf to have someone on the inside they could trust." She smirked.

The attitude on this woman was snatching my patience. I wanted to give her the benefit of the doubt by allowing her the chance to clear her name. Granted, we broke into her house, although she was definitely a bad apple that had to be dealt with. I fished in my pocket for some zip ties and bound her to the chair. This would conserve my energy while I went through her drawer to find proof of just how deep the rabbit hole went. The cabinet across the room stood out, and I realised that we didn't check it during the first visit. Surprisingly, it was unlocked. The first drawer showcased a blue folder that I cautiously opened, and for the second time in the past few hours, I was speechless. Photos filled each plastic pocket. Me and John, me and Andrew, Frank and Andrew, Ryan at Hotel Aldwych and some unknown people at dinner parties. The hell. This was getting interesting. I proceeded to look in the rest of the drawers, where I found a document binder with nefarious details on her colleagues. There was no way that this woman was working alone. She was under someone's thumb for sure. And she definitely wasn't on the right side of the law. And there it was every detail of my night with Mike. Pictures of us dancing in the club, proposals for his second visit that led to his death. "What the fuck?" My eyes narrowed as I read every sordid detail. Mike was working with the detective, and they were both involved in a colossal blackmailing ring. More bank statements surfaced with large cash deposits and withdrawals. I was flabbergasted.

"You see, hun, I have you and Frank by the balls. You can't do shit." Clearly, she didn't know me well enough.

The shadows of the trees swayed in the dim room. My heart raced, and my head started to pound. I called for Frank to come upstairs.

"Watch her. I'll be right back."

"What's happened?" I handed him the folders, and his face froze.

"Exactly."

"This is deep."

I left the room and sat at the top of the stairs to find clarity in the situation. At this point, I didn't know what I needed to do to make it all go away and perhaps it couldn't. Lord knows how many people were involved in this. I checked my watch, we had ten minutes, so I went back into the room.

"Frank, I need you to bring in some black bags." He looked puzzled but proceeded to exit the house to ask the guys for bags.

I crouched down in front of Detective Johnson and looked deep into her eyes to find part of myself in her. The part that needed to survive. Nonetheless, she and her wolf were plotting to ruin me, and I chose when to throw in the towel. For a split second, I saw hope and confidence flash on her face as though she had won. I looked around the room and remembered no signs of a family. No pictures or any items that indicated she cared for someone. I didn't even see the kitten's toys or food bowls. She didn't even realise he was gone. She lived in a state of neglect for herself, her house and her pet. What a waste of life. I took a moment to confirm my decision before I injected her with a second dose of the Vicodin solution. At this point, she was out of it, and the second injection released her from this world forever. I cut off the zip ties and stashed them in my pocket. By the time Frank arrived, her heart had stopped.

"You don't have to stay if you don't want to."

"Don't be ridiculous." It seemed that whatever he had been doing with Dr. Chris was helping him. Or maybe it was the fight we had the other night. Frank was no longer on edge. His head was in the game.

"Pack everything in this room in the bags. Don't leave behind a trace of her investigation. We'll make this look like an accidental overdose." Frank nodded. I wiped the syringe in her hand and left it on her desk while Frank quickly gathered all the files and photos. Five minutes left. I scrambled to help and paused when we heard footsteps on the landing. The Russian peeped inside the room.

"I thought you might need some help." Just in time. I instructed him to help us clear everything from the room, which we would later have time to analyse. When we were satisfied, we worked our way backwards, ensuring there were no traces of us which there wouldn't have been, but it was a good habit to be careful. We disposed of the gloves and shoe coverings as before and drove off.

My mind stilled as I counted backwards from ten. I needed to take a breath and get my shit together. Another mess ending (or beginning) with another murder. I looked at my hand and realised it had rolled into a tight fist. This wasn't my first time, but I had just discovered that Frank and I were caught up in a ring of lies.

"When you get home, drink a glass of whisky and sleep." I smiled, grateful at the Russian's attempt to make conversation. But, unfortunately, it was terrible timing. I needed silence. Frank looked a lot calmer than I did. Forty minutes later, we were perched on the sofa in my living room with Jules purring on Frank's lap.

I couldn't speak for Frank, but I was certainly exhausted. He took the Russian's advice and poured us both a stiff drink, smirking as he brought the glass to his lips.

"What?"

"Of all the absurdity today, you got yourself an admirer."

"Oh, stop it. He was just being nice."

"Izzy, I've known these guys for a long time. He has never uttered one word to me. I'm telling you, he's infatuated." Maybe he was infatuated though I had more significant problems on my plate. He was cute and had a nice body, like a street teddy bear. At that moment, I needed to take some time out. Frank made himself at home in my living room, setting up extra blankets and cushions for a cosy night's sleep. In the shower, my curls lathered and rinsed, I felt a weight lifted off my shoulders. Thoughts began to click, and it was a relief to feel like I was in control again. When I emerged in the living room, Frank had fallen asleep with Jules on his chest.

"Well, you're both cute." I whispered before retreating to my bedroom.

The sun beamed through the teal curtain, beckoning my consciousness from a deep sleep. It was morning, but my eyelids were still heavy, and my neck ached with tension from the tossing and turning the night before. I didn't fall into slumber until a mere few hours before dawn. It didn't matter because Frank and I were knee-deep in a sewer of games that, at this point, neither of us knew the rules. Images of the detective's face relaxing as she slipped into her void flashed in my mind. At first, I felt a pang of slow guilt creeping up my spine as I wondered if I killed her for nothing. Although after seeing the photos and documents, I was sure that she was someone I needed to take out of the picture before she did more damage. Then, I realised that there probably wasn't any official investigation into Mike's disappearance. If he was involved with the likes of Detective Johnson and everything was set up, he probably had no family missing him. Just the 'big bad wolf', as she put it. Questions danced in my head. Who were these people? Who else had eyes on us? Are the guys involved? Paranoia crept in. It didn't make sense that the Russian began chatting to me as though he wanted to make friends. I trusted no one. I simply couldn't.

In the kitchen, the clock presented 9 a.m. taunting me to climb back into bed for another hour. Frank and Jules stirred on the sofa as I poured food into his bowl. I had no idea how to look after a kitten or any pet for that matter, but there was no way I was going to leave Jules in that filthy house, starving for food and love. Yes, Frank and I were criminals, but we would never allow an animal to suffer. I turned on the kettle and made us both a cup of tea. By the time I rummaged in the fridge for some breakfast, Jules was at his bowl scoffing food, and Frank yawned from the sofa.

"Turkey sausage and pancakes for breakfast." I announced from the kitchen.

"Yum, I might have to move in." Frank beamed. He proceeded to the bathroom while I cooked breakfast. Every action was mechanical and emotionless, with a to-do list reciting in my head. Register Jules with the vet, clean the apartment, organise the photos and documents, call Nathan. I had forgotten about Nathan since Frank showed up, and I kicked him out.

Breakfast was consumed in silence while I worked on my next move. First, I organised my bookings with clients for the following month, and when we finished eating, I got myself ready to bring Jules to the local vet. Frank decided to accompany me so that we could talk about our findings from the detective's house.

"At the moment, it's in our best interest to lay low." He whispered as we sat at the reception. The room was empty, but such a topic of conversation had to be spoken with care.

"I agree, but we can't keep waiting for people to come and surprise us. Aren't you curious to know who is running this ring?"

"Of course I am, but I also want to stay alive and out of prison." He had a point. The last thing I wanted was for neither of us to be in the deep end of trouble that led us to prison or dead, especially with our birthdays around the corner.

Chapter Ten

Isabella

It was finally here. My birthday. It was a day celebrated with family and friends for everyone else. Since I only had Frank, we decided to smoke, eat Japanese food and drink our body weight in bourbon. We had no responsibilities other than ourselves, our money and Jules, who had now settled into his new home with ease. Frank, being the kind-hearted man he was, bought loads of toys, the finest kitten food and velvet blankets that money could buy to ensure our new little friend was comfortable and at peace. We learned that the kitten loved to sleep, which was fine since we planned to have fun. The autumn air had settled into a thick fog that hid the rest of the city below us while the temperature dropped to the coldest it had been during the year. Frank's birthday was four days before mine, so we decided to keep the momentum of indulgence going until we had both turned twenty-eight. Unlike the previous birthdays where we partied the nights away in clubs, we decided to stay in and have fun in peace.

Even before meeting Frank, my birthday had been somewhat depressing for the beginning of my adult life. When I first moved to the city and had no one to share the *special* day with, I chugged a bottle of beer and bought myself the best instant noodle I could afford until I made enough money working for Tom who's family took a liking to making me feel like one of their own. Still, I hated the feeling of reliance. I hated being in debt to people even though they convinced me otherwise. I was grateful to Tom and his family nonetheless, and every now and then, I lent them a thought. I missed them, but life went on. It was best to detach and keep pushing forward. Frank was hilariously tipsy, and I couldn't remember a time seeing him like that with his guard down. His attention focused on Jules' well-being the entire time, almost exhibiting the characteristics of an obsessive parent. I, on the other hand, nibbled my way through the mountain of food we ordered.

"So, have you called him lately?" I blurted the question without caution. It was a question that nagged at me since I found out Frank was in contact with Ryan. Since then, I, too, wondered if he was okay, although I couldn't get over how he left me many months ago.

"No. If I did, I would tell you. Lesson learned." I felt bad for how I reacted, but at the moment, my reaction was justified. Other people lied to each other, Frank and I lied to other people, but we were past lying to each other. Especially when we were both entangled in the largest web of lies of our lives. I continued to nibble on the tempura, focusing my senses on the present rather than what was or could've been. Fuck Ryan.

By the late evening, frank had fallen into a deep sleep despite reassuring that he was only resting his eyes. I knew better since he had smoked until his pupils dilated black and his muscles relaxed on the sofa like he was spending the day at a spa. I decided to take the time for some self-reflection. I'm that moment, I was grateful for Frank and the people I'd met during the past few months. It must've been the bourbon. Yes, I'm definitely blaming the alcohol. Somehow I found myself dialling Nathan's number. There was no explanation for the pull between us. Without hesitation, he arrived at my apartment just before midnight.

"It's your birthday, and you didn't tell me?" I would've brought you something nice.

Just like that, we were once again doing the routine dance of our lust, entwined into each other's arms, skin glued with sweat on one another. There was no need to talk about our arrangement. Something inside me knew that if I had a friend with benefits situation with anyone, it would be Nathan. He wasn't the friend that Frank was to me, but I allowed myself to care about him. And it was apparent that he cared about me too. Oh, stop it, Izzy. I shook myself out of the thought. Nathan wasn't a great romantic match for my chaos. He was different. Maybe it was in a good way.

In the morning, I awoke to the smell of chemicals and the sound of the vacuum. There was no way Frank would be cleaning. I unlocked the bedroom door to find Nathan packing away the last bin bags. He cleaned. And Frank sat at the kitchen island, nursing a hangover. He looked dishevelled and bloated.

"You look positively ghastly, sir." I teased as I slid on the seat next to him. He clutched onto the cup of coffee for dear life. Nathan approached us with a smile on his face. The doorbell rang, and he leapt to answer.

Moments later, he came back into the living room with a large box and a large bouquet of flowers. Frank acted like he didn't know what was happening and focused his eyes on my perplexed gaze that was tainted with a hint of embarrassment. I wasn't good with surprises. The box was displayed on the coffee table and opened. Inside was the most extravagant birthday cake I had ever seen with sparkly gold icing.

"It's vanilla," Frank whispered, knowing that I would eat no other flavour. My mouth curved with the goofiest smile.

"Oh my goodness, thank you so much."

"It was Frank's idea. And you deserve it." I looked over at Frank, rolling his eyes trying to act cool, but I knew that he loved the sentiment. "This was my idea." The bouquet of pink roses with embellished satin ribbons he presented was all it took to make my eyes glaze with moisture. I never had a man be this thoughtful on my birthday. It was a simple gesture, but it meant a lot. I had my fair share of expensive gifts throughout my adult life. However, this gesture was associated with gentleness, and Nathan expected nothing in return.

The rest of the day was spent chit-chatting about life, sipping wine and embracing friendship. I wasn't sure if this was a lasting relationship for Nathan and me, although I was willing to accept him in my life for as long as he wanted.

"Your kitten is cute. When did you get him?" Nathan announced, prompting Frank and I to exchange a smirky glance at each other.

"Oh, a few days ago. We adopted him."

"That's when you had the emergency." He baited.

"Yeah, our friend rescued him." I responded, holding back the need to further explain. I didn't feel bad withholding information since if he knew every aspect of my life, he would run a mile, have a heart attack or run to the police. I hoped he stayed in ignorance for as long as possible. Otherwise, I would have to kill him if he ran to the police.

The autumn months flew by and wrapped us in a whirlwind of cosiness. Frank was busy with work. Nathan and his brother celebrated the opening of the second restaurant that doubled in profit, leaving their investors and their own bank accounts beaming. The dust had settled on Detective Johnson's murder, and as usual, nothing surfaced in the news, nor did we receive unexpected visitors. Jules had grown into a playful ball of fur and had taken a liking to Nathan. Frank, however, was forever his favourite person. It was a sunny Thursday afternoon when I decided to stop by the local café for my usual chai latte and a pastry when a distinguished man approached my table. He didn't have to say much, as I noticed him when he paid for his coffee at the counter.

"I love the pastries here." The Russian said in his rough voice. I still couldn't get over how comfortable he felt talking to me. It was strange, and I was wary of his sudden interest to make friends.

"Yeah, it is. How have you been?" I moved my bag from the empty chair and encouraged him to sit down. At first, he hesitated, then relented. I knew how to read people, especially men who felt the need to test my patience. After a few minutes of small talk, he felt comfortable telling me his name was Mikhail but preferred to be called Mik. That was reassuring, but I wasn't wholly convinced. The chat was light, but eventually, he announced that he had to leave. There was no mention of his work or the events that occurred the last time we saw each other. He didn't even mention the kitten. Back at home, I told Frank about the encounter.

"Well, maybe he did just want a chat with a pretty woman. I bet he doesn't have any normal friends. Did he say anything to you that made you feel uncomfortable?"

"No, he was really nice."

"Well, what's the problem then?" Frank had checked out from the moment he took the first hit of his vape.

"That's exactly the problem. He was *too* nice." We continued with the back and forth, debating on Mik's character but eventually settled on proceeding with caution. These evening rituals of conversation, sipping our favourite tipple while planning world domination, had become frequent for us, and if we weren't in my apartment, I was at Frank's. Although, I knew that he preferred to stay a mine's since I had better snacks.

By the time the first snow fell, it was Christmas morning. To everyone else, Christmas was a magical day, but for us, it was just another time of year to drink wine, eat good food and plot. This time though, Nathan was also sharing our time with Frank's new friend Mik. So imagine the surprise on my face when I accidentally walked in on him and Frank having sex in Frank's living room. It turned out that he made friendly conversation with me because he was too shy to speak to Frank, whom he's had a crush on since the day they met, but it was never the right time to make a move. I was relieved, though, that the sudden interest in conversation was to get closer to Frank. The rest of the guys, however, were still the same. Only speaking to us when necessary, being careful not to utter more than a friendly hello when called upon for their services. Mik didn't have family beyond the people he worked with, and like us, he was just trying to survive with the hand that life had dealt him. Frank insisted that were nothing more than two people just infatuated with each other, even though they were very much exhibiting couple behaviour. They had met on a night out, having a one night's stand that continued into Christmas morning. As long as Frank were happy, I was happy.

When the snow settled over the city, we all wrapped up in our warm coats, sharing a joint on my balcony, heckling the passersby as they skidded on the icy pavements. Eventually, the darkness settled, prompting us to eat dinner and settle in the cosiness of the warmth that emitted from our friendships and Jules, who was bouncing with playful energy. We weren't a conventional family, but it was the perfect ushering into a year's ending.

"A toast to new beginnings." Nathan announced as we dug into our turkey. I wasn't sure if the new beginning would last for us, but I hoped for the best.

"To new beginnings!" I mirrored and raised my glass while the rest chimed in. We were tipsy and giddy until we halted at the rustling sound that came from the front door. Frank and Mik were at their feet with instincts, ready to fight the intruder. Within a few seconds, the door unlocked and as Frank got ready to charge but stopped in his track when he saw the familiar face peek through. Ryan. There he was, the man who fought as hard as he fucked, the part of me I thought I lost forever. My heart leapt to him, but my body remained rigid. The room blurred as our eyes met, and I grabbed a mental picture of his muscular frame. He was still handsome, alluring and dark. Nathan uttered a few words that I couldn't make out. Sweat beaded off my forehead while I stood, frozen beyond time.

END.

Books by J.P. Mooney

A Virgo's Point of You
Prose for those seeing the world for what it truly is
The Ups and Downs of Winning Series, Book Three

F*CK You, I'm Tired
Prose for navigating the politics of life
The Ups and Downs of Winning Series, Book Two

F*CK You, I'm Fabulous
Prose for the bold
The Ups and Downs of Winning Series, Book One

Beautiful Jaded Butterflies:
Sometimes love is nothing but a twisted game of chess *Mated Fortune Series, Book Two*

Isabella:
Crime has never looked this fabulous *Mated Fortune Series, Book One*

Ley Lines
Poetry for the certified warrior

tiny reads:
A poetry collection for on the go spirits

Prana: Poems of the Moment

Virgo's Carousel:
Are you brave enough for the ride?

Mercury Retrograde Poems: Climbing off the Ferris Wheel

<u>Available on Amazon</u>

9 781838 035181